PIERRE PÉJU

The Girl from
the Chartreuse

TRANSLATED FROM THE FRENCH BY
Ina Rilke

VINTAGE BOOKS
London

3451607

Published by Vintage 2006

2 4 6 8 10 9 7 5 3 1

First published with the title *La petite Chartreuse* in 2002
by Gallimard, Paris

First published in Great Britain in 2005 by The Harvill Press

Vintage
Random House, 20 Vauxhall Bridge Road,
London SW1V 2SA

Random House Australia (Pty) Limited
20 Alfred Street, Milsons Point, Sydney,
New South Wales 2061, Australia

Random House New Zealand Limited
18 Poland Road, Glenfield, Auckland 10, New Zealand

Random House (Pty) Limited
Isle of Houghton, Corner of Boundary Road & Carse O'Gowrie,
Houghton, 2198, South Africa

The Random House Group Limited Reg. No. 954009
www.randomhouse.co.uk/vintage

A CIP catalogue record for this book
is available from the British Library

Ouvrage traduit avec le concours du Ministère Français chargé de la
culture – Centre National du Livre.
This work is published with support from the French Ministry of
Culture – Centre National du Livre.
This book is supported by the French Ministry of Foreign Affairs,
as part of the Burgess Programme headed for the French Embassy in
London by the Institut Français du Royaume-Uni

ïi institut français

ISBN 9780099468691 (from Jan 2007)
ISBN 0099468697

Printed and bound in Great Britain by
Cox & Wyman Ltd, Reading, Berkshire

CONTENTS

Publisher's Note

The Massif de la Chartreuse is in south-eastern France, in the Rhônes-Alpes region. Its name derives from the first Carthusian monastery founded there in 1084 and called "La Grande Chartreuse".

The title of the novel in French is *La petite Chartreuse*, meaning "The Little Carthusian Nun". Members of the Carthusian Order take a vow of silence.

PART I

A Child Run Over

Five in the afternoon. It will be exactly five in the afternoon under the bitter cold November rain when the van of the bookseller Vollard (Étienne) spurting down the avenue collides head-on with a little girl who runs smack into his path.

Frail limbs, pale, tender flesh beneath red anorak and tights, the little girl lunges forward. Eyes misting with tears, the panic of a lost child, and, in that final split second, the look of terror under the brown fringe. Sprung from nowhere, the small body is pitched in the air on impact. It rolls over the bonnet, forehead slammed against the windscreen, and Vollard thinks he can hear the sound of bone cracking in the screech of his brakes. In the roar and growl of rush-hour traffic is this child, struck down in mid-flight, scooped up, rolled over, then flung way back, the satchel plucked away, one shoe gone.

On the soaking asphalt a dark-red puddle slowly spreads around a body like a broken doll and rivulets of blood go snaking between the tyres of cars screaming to a halt in the November rain.

It will be five in the afternoon, but for the moment the accident has not taken place. Nor is it fated to happen, for there is no writing on the wall, or anywhere else for that matter, just life riddled with last-minute contingencies, the kind of little nothings that, for all the direness of their consequences, defy foresight or precaution.

In every neighbourhood of every city and town, half-past four is the time when children get out of their elementary schools. They call it "mothers' time". The long streets lined with grey buildings, deserted only moments ago, come alive with a jolly hubbub punctuated by children's shrill cries; schools open up like shells, and beneath their cloth carapaces drummed by the rain, the mothers flock to welcome their little ones hobbled by satchels bumping in the throng.

Looming, hurried mothers stoop over children raising soft little snouts, offering smooth cheeks, all clamouring for attention, brandishing handiwork confectioned out of cardboard, fabric and clay. Strong maternal tentacles relieve drooping shoulders of their burdens and store away precious objects, and all of a sudden the mêlée is breaking up, umbrellas making off already in all directions. A revving of engines and swift family getaways.

The woman in the blue smock, trailing children who will be collected later, comes out to shut the school gate.

Silence falls once more, lights are switched off, the rain intensifies.

Anything can happen now, including the worst. The worst is merely one among a host of possibilities, a hyena lurking among ambient trivia.

At half-past four Éva, the little girl in the red anorak, joins the stream of children crossing the courtyard. Once outside the gate, ranks are joyfully broken. In the pack of mothers, each child is immediately capable of singling out the distinctive, familiar warmth that is theirs, the hand in which to slip their own, the cheek upon which to plant a rapid kiss. The aroma of motherhood, of moist sweetness, of a brioche after school. Little daily, rainy encounters.

In the surging crowd Éva drags her feet while the others press ahead. She can feel the heavy raindrops slithering down her fringe on to her forehead. She's a new pupil at this school, new in the neighbourhood, even the town is new to her. She has hardly spoken to her schoolmates yet.

Éva is anxious, as she is every afternoon. She dreads not seeing her mother in the waiting throng, dreads not finding a pair of fond eyes meeting her own, drawing her near.

Éva's mother is so often late! Might be a few minutes, but sometimes a lot more, and it has been like that ever since they came to live in this town. Most days it is only after the mothers have disappeared in all directions that Thérèse turns up. Hurrying, short of breath, a cigarette between her fingers. From afar she flutters a hand in a vague gesture of explanation, shakes her head and smiles as if to implore her child's forgiveness before resuming her expression of hazy detachment.

Day after day the young mother says things like "I was held up for ages . . . Éva, you understand, don't you, pet?" Or murmurs, with mock indignation: "This is outrageous! Did they let you out early?" as if she didn't know perfectly well that the school opens and closes its shell like clockwork.

But until now this wayward mother has always turned up eventually. That's all that counts for Éva, that's what stops things from spinning round and making her dizzy, what keeps the very ground in this town where she doesn't know a soul from flying away from beneath her feet.

On the way home the child clings to her mother's coat, the mother who shrinks from holding hands, as if a small hand slipped between her tobacco-stained fingers would be an encumbrance, an embarrassment.

On this day Éva feels more and more wretched amid the soggy raincoats and dripping umbrellas. Her heart thumps painfully as she screws up her eyes to scan the far end of the street, hoping to make out the only mother that matters. But no. Nothing but shapes moving away from her. No-one remotely resembling her mother. The silence settles like a thickening fog. The school gate is locked, and as Éva didn't dare ask the woman in the blue smock if she could stay with her, she can only huddle in the entranceway for shelter. Anxiously, she rises on tiptoe, quivering like a hunted animal, then squats down: a sad, resigned red frog. With a sigh she draws herself up again, scratches her ankle. She knows she can't find her way home from school: the flat they moved into only two months ago is too far away.

Éva's dark eyes search more and more rapidly in all directions.

This time she has heard her own voice say "Maman". Each passer-by turns out to be agonisingly unfamiliar when seen up close. That's her, over there! No, it's not her.

The misery of waiting around on this cold pavement, with spreading puddles and a crumpled newspaper soaking in the gutter, fills her with a sense of being nothing, of being invisible.

Suddenly the small figure breaks away from her shelter and flees. Éva, a wisp of a girl, runs across town with her satchel heavy with books bumping against the small of her back. The pavements are slippery. Tail-lights make big red stars in her tear-filled eyes, blurring her vision. If it weren't for the rumble of the city you'd hear the anguish pouring from her throat as she dashes across a street, then another, without slowing her pace, without looking left or right, then a third and a fourth, as they come.

Éva runs as fast as she can, her lungs bursting. Parched throat, aching legs, slowed down by that sack of a satchel, which she would love to discard except that to have lost it would be even worse.

The accident hasn't happened yet. The slightest shift in circumstances and it would never take place. Éva could have been, miraculously, taking the right road home, she could have collapsed exhausted in a doorway until someone noticed her and said, "Are you lost, little one?" But none of these things come to pass, and the cold rain doesn't help either.

Éva follows her headlong trajectory, not knowing that at that very moment her mother, having taken a massive dose of oblivion, a double dose of pure indifference, is nevertheless now speeding towards her. But she is still much too far away to get to the school in time.

[7]

★ ★

Not far away, likewise braving the downpour, Étienne Vollard is pursuing his own trajectory. The two lines will intersect at a singular, tragic point.

On his own as usual, he is driving his green van chock-a-block with books in cardboard boxes. Vollard is so large, so tall and so solid that even with his seat tilted as far back as it will go, getting his paunch and thighs behind the steering wheel is a very tight fit. Six hundred kilos of hardware, two hundred kilos of books, one hundred and ten kilos of Vollard, in short, a mass of mechanical, human and literary goods weighing a ton, rolling down the four-lane avenue that bisects the town from north to south. The bookseller drives on automatic pilot, muttering under his breath: ". . . *the general outline of despair. Despair has no heart, my hand always touches breathless despair, the despair whose mirrors never tell us if it is dead.*"

Vollard is not a keen driver, he isn't one for speed of any kind, but he needs his van to transport the stocks of old or second-hand books that he sometimes goes quite a distance to buy, so he occasionally finds himself caught up in the always too fast traffic on the avenues.

That evening road surfaces are slippery, vehicles whip up great sprays of water, windscreen wipers work overtime. Éva is still running on the side road parallel to the avenue, stumbling, bumping into people and metal or concrete barriers, grazing a knee.

So it is that she decides to cross the avenue. There seems

no end to it and she has been running alongside it for a while. A thundering, raging flood. Panting, she squeezes between the bumpers of the cars parked on the side, then plunges headlong, not looking about her, seeing nothing, into the roiling current.

A fraction of a second too late, bookseller Étienne Vollard sees the tiny figure leaping into the yellowish, rain-streaked beam of his headlights. Every muscle in him contracts; he is seized with terror. Brake pedal slammed, steering wheel wrenched to the left, Vollard clinging, straining with all his might as though he could, with his own bare hands, still prevent the iron monster from goring its victim. Too late . . . The wheels lock in an unstoppable skid. Vollard, van, and volumes fuse together in a compacted mass bearing down on the little girl, scooping her off the asphalt, tossing her up. A first muffled shock, then the thud of the body against the windscreen, then the air filling with screeching brakes, blasts of noise and more thuds in a pandemonium that seems to go on for ever.

In flashes Vollard sees the little red anorak, the pallor, the wide-eyed terror, two huge, disbelieving eyes fleetingly locked with his. For a long time afterwards he is convinced that this is what he actually saw through his windscreen: the child's face separated from his own old face only by the glass against which it is about to be slammed.

Time freezes solid, stopped at pure horror. Vollard is immured in his seat, hands soldered to the wheel. A dead weight.

Bookseller in the Snow

With a supreme effort he succeeds in stirring himself, to open the door of the van, but in his struggle to heave himself out of the driver's seat his feet get caught in the safety-belt, which he never uses and which hangs beside his seat. He tumbles heavily to his knees, hands flat on the sticky asphalt, and advances on all fours towards the body he can see lying a few metres away pinned in the headlights of cars stuck fast all round him. Everything seems plunged into a deathly hush.

Reaching the body, his head explodes with the cacophony of an improbable thousand-man orchestra all tuning up at once, and he freezes. He stares at the inert little heap lying before him: a slip of a child, the head strangely twisted, the arms unjointed, one red foot shoeless. Holding his breath, he leans forward over the half-closed eyes, the mouth contorted and bleeding, the skin horribly pale, the blood. Hands flat on the ground, his eyes follow the trickle of creamy-red liquid winding through the burnt black rubber skid marks.

Now the orchestra crashes all around him – shrieks, blaring trumpets, clashing cymbals – and Vollard becomes aware of a dark, angry crowd gathering overhead. Soon he is being punched, pulled about. People try to drag him up off the ground, away from the object of his fascination. He keeps wanting to say: "She's still breathing, she's bleeding, still breathing . . ." but he has lost his voice. As in a dream, he does not feel the punches and kicks against his shanks, nor the hands pulling his hair and tugging at his clothing – how heavy he is! In the end it takes several men to seize him, plant him upright. They are police officers. Already an ambulance is there, sirens howling, the blue revolving beam lighting fitfully on spectral bystanders. A woman has retrieved the child's satchel, the tiny missing shoe. "She's still breathing . . ." he mouths, but his voice is flat, breathless, dying.

Sitting opposite him in the police van, a very young police officer looks at him, calmly asks him questions. There is a smell of wet leather, stale sweat, tobacco. Vollard gets a grip of himself, checks whether he is still wearing his glasses, wipes his hands on his trousers. He says very clearly: "She jumped out in front of me, she just jumped out . . ." and then he rambles on. He accepts without argument to breathe into the plastic tube that is held out to him, blows noisily into it when asked to blow, signs everything he is asked to sign, hunts dutifully in his pockets for the required documents. Eye-witnesses describe what they saw to a second officer, just as young, just as calm as the first.

The officers and witnesses get out of the police van, leaving Vollard behind. He has seen the stretcher, heard the ambulance siren wailing, and tells himself that if they're in such a hurry to get the child to hospital it must mean that she isn't dead, that she isn't going to die . . . He watches through the barred window as policemen with flashlights inspect his van, discover the spill of books in the back. Traffic has started up again: the noise of engines drowns out the voices.

There is no doubt in Vollard's mind that he will be taken into custody, he cannot imagine that he will not be. The young officer, now dripping wet, climbs back into the dimly lit vehicle, shielding his papers with a piece of plastic.

"You can go," he says to Vollard. "The report is finished . . . Vehicle in sound condition . . . negative alcohol test . . . According to all the witnesses there wasn't much you could do. The child was in a total panic . . . didn't look where she was going, jumped right under your wheels . . . You'll receive a summons later, there will be an inquiry. You'll have to testify. But for now, you're free to go."

"And the child, is she going to be all right?"

"Look, they've taken her to Emergency at the hospital, they'll do what they can . . . Sadly, we see this every day of the week."

Vollard gets down from the police van. Adjusting his glasses which are already spotting in the rain, he feels a tap on his shoulder. It is the young officer: "Here, you forgot the keys to your van!" He is going to have to get behind the wheel again.

The police van has gone. The crowd has dispersed. It is not rain coming down in sheets, it is acid solitude, a corrosive fog isolating Vollard from the rest of existence. His hands are shaking, he has trouble putting the key into the ignition.

[12]

Finally the engine splutters to life. The van carrying its deadweight of books lurches forward, exactly as before, but Vollard, terrified of another collision, doesn't dare resume his journey down the avenue at a normal speed. Cars sound their horns in protest. He turns into a side street at random, then another, ears pounding with the flat, dull, shattering sound of a child's body being smashed against the bonnet, against the windscreen, the crunch of bone, the squeal of brakes, and a sense of everything skidding hopelessly out of control. Hands gripping the steering wheel, clamped on the atrocity. Every muscle in his leg, his thigh, slamming the brake.

And so he drives, Vollard the bookseller, trapped in this reverie of death. He signals, turns on to the dim-lit wharfs, straight through a red light.

There is more hooting, but traffic is thinning, making way for more emptiness and gathering gloom. Before long he is in the outskirts, on a road sweeping steeply up the mountain beyond the last, big, tight-packed houses.

This is one of the city's attractions: one minute you're cruising along boulevards teeming with people, all around you office blocks, high-rise flats and department stores, and the next you find yourself quite alone on a mountainside, in a place that is still wild.

Then come the first bends, a sharp incline rising to a succession of hairpins among rocky outcrops. Stray stones have rolled down on to the road. Vollard drives at a snail's pace, as though about to pull up to survey the twinkle of lights down below, the yellow streak of the avenue where the accident happened, the illuminated blocks of the large hospital where they must have taken the little girl, the blue neons, the moving headlamps, the traffic lights switching from red to green all over the city enfolded by the massing heights of the mountains.

But now Vollard can't stop; he weaves his way on across deserted villages, vales, forests of fir trees. Down in the sodden valley the city evaporates, magically effaced by the might of the mountains. The rain turns to molten snow and then, as he gains altitude, to whirling snowflakes.

The road is steadily steeper, but narrower too, until it is little more than a slit in the dense forest, where the risk of getting lost or vanishing from the face of the earth seems real. The van climbs incredibly slowly, as if it is falling asleep and barely capable of making any headway at all. Upon reaching a crest it gives up, spent with fatigue, in the middle of the road. Vollard opens the door, lets the flakes settle on him in silence. Everything is swathed in white, a snowy veil draped on the branches, crisp lace on the grassy verges, silvery hoarfrost lighting up the gloom.

On the edge of a large clearing, a hotel closed for the season. Blacked-out windows in the forest night. Abandoned snow ploughs. Tree trunks stacked up like dead giants under a shroud. Further on the road plunges down again into the depths of the forest and yet another valley.

Once he has extricated his hulking mass, Vollard stands in

the night air, raises his head to the sky, and starts walking. He shoves his fists in his pockets. The cold bites his face, his shoulders.

At first the road feels like a soft carpet underfoot, then it turns into a forest trail white with older, harder snow as he trudges on, dodging low branches and knotty roots, barely able to see where he is going. A footpath dies out among the boulders. Vollard stumbles several times, but climbs on, unthinking, stooping now and then to grab hold of anything he can use to heave himself on and up – jutting, frozen rocks, razor-sharp grasses, rough, coral-hard lichen. Arriving at a glade with powdered, brittle shrubs around a bed of frozen mud and wavy snow formations, Vollard pauses. The sparse snowflakes seem to be falling in slow motion. He stands stock-still. The sound of his breathing fills the air, which smells of damp bark. He clenches his fists, fills his lungs and begins to scream.

The scream is hoarse, unending, terrible. Carrying far into the night. Like a beast in blackest agony. Like bile spewed up from some gigantic belly. A scream that takes a long time to ebb away, only to return with renewed anguish. A scream on the mountain, rising up over the treetops and the boulders, even higher, soaring to the summits bursting into the black seal of sky. As Vollard lets out his powerful cry, the world around him holds its breath, shrinks away. Not a murmur from the animals hiding in their lairs, huddled together in hollows, nothing but this cry in the November night.

Never for an instant does his scream turn to tears. Vollard

is incapable of shedding tears. He only howls to the point of exhaustion. He waits for a long time before setting off again, sinking to his knees in a creamy bank of snow, then ploughing through tangled brushwood, stumbling over hidden stones on his path, bent double, arms outstretched before him. He yearns to stride across the forest, charge up the mountain like an antediluvian beast, a powerhouse of strength, but he keeps running into thick, dead branches which break off against his forehead, and he can't tell if it is melted snow trickling down his cheeks, or sweat, or blood.

Losing his balance, he falls awkwardly against a sawn-off tree trunk, fears he has cracked some ribs. Painfully, he scrambles to his feet and staggers on in a daze, delivering wild, random blows with his fists to the trees as he passes, but suddenly the ground falls away and he loses his footing again. This time he topples over and his massive body slithers down the slope, comes to a halt in a mess of snow and frozen mud.

His hands and feet are numb. His forehead and his ribs ache, but, strangely, the pain acts as a sort of safeguard in his bewilderment. His coat is soaked through and the icy clamminess gnaws at the skin of his old, tough carcass. The ground underfoot feels more or less level, and he follows what he takes to be a track. No longer bothering to hold out his arms, he improvises his route in the dark.

The track leads him further down, a ravine in a nightmare. He has exhausted his need to cry out. He pulls himself together, steadies himself. Inhales hard, listens to the night. The silence is overwhelming. There must be animals out

[16]

there, deep in their winter sleep, oblivious to this intrusive suffering.

Only now does he realise that he is shaking in all his limbs, his teeth are chattering uncontrollably. But the deep-seated dread has lifted. He knows he is not going to die tonight, that he won't even catch a cold as long as he keeps moving. He knows how much reserve energy is stored in the core of his vast frame. His fall just now is nothing compared to what he has been through. Losing his way like this, being in pain and tramping in the darkness of this mountain which he has come to know so well, helps him to face up to what he will have to live with henceforth: the unconscionable outrage of having run over and maybe killed a child.

Vollard limps and shivers in the silence, but his old mental strength returns. After a time he finds himself on a small mountain road.

He pushes on, hugging himself and beating his arms to keep the circulation going, but the icy cold gets the better of him and he trembles convulsively. Daybreak is interminably long in coming.

The road rises gently, and as he rounds a slight bend he can make out the outline of a substantial house even darker than the surroundings, the yellowish square of a lighted window, a smell of smoke. There is a man standing at the door, holding something. Motionless, he watches as Vollard detaches himself from the night, approaches and stops a few paces short of the door. Close by, a dog lets out a long growl. The man seems neither surprised nor distrustful. He puts down his bucket, and the clatter of metal on stone rouses Vollard from his stupor. He wants to speak, greet the man, explain himself, but not a sound passes his lips. The man notes Vollard's mud-encrusted hair, the bleeding forehead, the ripped trousers and jacket.

"Has there been an accident?" he inquires evenly.

"Yes," stammers Vollard, shivering. "An accident . . . "

"Come in and get warm, anyway, get yourself together. You're shaking badly. Was anyone else involved? Anyone injured?"

"I was alone . . . There is no-one else. I am alone . . . "

"Here, I've just made some coffee, it's pretty hot. Help yourself."

He is somewhat taken aback by the sheer size of the stranger: lost, wet, bruised and bleeding, a good head taller than he is.

Instinctively, Vollard moves towards the stove. The dog sniffs at his legs, rears up and scratches at the drenched trousers. On the wall there is a calendar with a picture of a fire engine for the month of November. Still tongue-tied but beginning to thaw, Vollard fastens his eyes on the red blur of the fire engine.

"Emergency service," the man says, pointing his chin towards the calendar and tapping the mobile phone clipped to his belt. "I can call them if you like."

"No, there's no need," says Vollard, his hands curled around the steaming coffee cup. "It's all right . . ."

"What about the accident? Your car?"

[18]

"The accident was yesterday. It wasn't here, it was down in the valley. I've been walking all night. I needed to walk . . . I fell a couple of times, no bones broken, though, I don't think . . ."

He grimaces with pain.

"Cracked ribs at the most, but it could be worse. I was trying to find where I'd left my van, but I seem to have got lost. Is there a mountain pass somewhere near here?"

"So it's yours, is it, that abandoned van up at the top? Not even locked. I noticed it yesterday evening when I was out with the dog. I was puzzled . . . I thought something must have happened to the driver. But instead of a dead body I found all those books. Good Lord! So many books! If you follow the road uphill for a good kilometre you'll find it. It's the pass. But you'd better wait until the day breaks. *If* it breaks . . . "

"No, I'll go now. Thanks for the coffee, for letting me get warm. I'd best be off. I'm still wet, but at least I'm not shaking any more."

"Tell me, what do you do with all those books?"

"I read them. Buy them. Sell them, too. Live with them. Thanks again, but I must be getting back . . . I'll be fine."

"As you like," the man says. "You know, I've lived here a very long time. And my father and my grandfather before me, born and bred in the Chartreuse. So you can bet that we've seen our share of people like you, turning up out of the blue at all sorts of hours. Plenty of them. It's the mountain that does it."

[19]

"I'm not surprised," Vollard replies.

"It's always the same. Whenever someone shows up in the dead of night or in the early hours, it's always because something has happened to them elsewhere. They've had an accident, some sorrow or some terrible news. So they come here, from miles away sometimes. It's the pull of the Chartreuse. Always the same . . . They climb the way you climbed, I'm not saying deliberately to get lost, but rather to lose themselves awhile. It's been going on for centuries. In the beginning there were monks, hermits, nutters, and, to be sure, poor sods like you . . . although you, I must say . . ." The man hesitates . . .

"Well?" asks Vollard.

"I can't speak for my father, but for myself, I never saw anyone as big as you, as . . ."

"As broad in the beam? I know, I get in the way. I've been getting in my own way for a long time. That's how it is. Anyway, thanks again."

Vollard sets off in the direction of the pass. The dog comes with him for a while, trotting from left to right, sniffing the tracks of wild creatures, marking territory a few times in the snow before turning tail.

When the bookseller gets his van going again and winds down to the city, it is snowing in the mountains. The peaks have vanished behind a herd of elephantine clouds. It is snowing on the frozen rocks, making their white blankets deeper. It is snowing on the dusky meadows, on the wooded slopes of the Chartreuse mountains, on the winding road which turns into a strip of felt, on the monasteries secreted in the folds of the foothills. It is snowing on the tombs of monks dead for centuries, on the city, the slippery avenues, its towers, its bridges, its parks, and it is snowing on the big hospital where they took the little girl. Thick flakes settle on the picture windows of the municipal library, over the bricked-up windows of the morgue. Black flakes in the glow of streetlamps. White flakes in the unlit alleys.

In the flurry of snow Vollard is utterly alone. Every fibre of his being is frozen, brittle. Jaws clamped, clenched fists. He decides to go to Emergency as soon as possible. With each hairpin bend he gets a better look at the grey sprawl of the city below. The hospital looms into view, a city within a city, where pain and suffering, injuries, diseases and agonies are packed on to every huge level.

Passing through the glass doors Vollard feels he is entering a labyrinth. He pauses in the onslaught of medicinal smells, squeaking stretcher trolleys laden with newly injured, prostrate bodies, the bustle of white coats and dressings. He leans over the visitors' desk, trying not to intimidate the receptionist. Why would this dishevelled, haggard stranger who doesn't look too well himself wish to inquire after a child brought in the previous evening?

He talks quickly, in a hoarse voice: "Could you please check . . . It happened yesterday afternoon, just after five. A little girl . . . run over by a van."

"Well, monsieur, you say you were notified, and you can't tell me her name? Are you family?

"Yes I am . . ."

By the glass doors, a male nurse is going off duty, but hesitates, cursing at the heavy snow, then turns back to the reception.

"He probably means the kid run over, yesterday afternoon. About ten years old. They took her up to the theatre . . . she was in a hell of a bad way . . ."

The nurse is tired and wants to go home, but Vollard persists: "She wasn't . . .?"

"Dead? No, when she was brought in she was still breathing. They must have tried surgery. That's all I know, you'll have to ask upstairs . . ."

And so, having put the sombre forest, the mountain and the snow behind him, Vollard is about to penetrate the deepest recesses of the regional hospital where he will finally learn what has become of the child whose terrified eyes he can still see locked with his own. He knows full well, in his muscles and flesh and bones and nerves and brain, that the evening with snow in the air will never end, that he will go on and on colliding with the small body for the rest of his days.

Transparent Woman

Thérèse is driving at high speed. A washed-out landscape hurls itself at her face. Windscreen wipers mew in synch. She's driving too fast, but not fast enough to arrive at her daughter's school at going-home time. Éva will be waiting. The steering wheel vibrates in her clenched hands, but Thérèse remains strangely calm. She keeps telling herself how important it is to be on time. She knows you can't abandon a child that has no-one in the world but its mother. She tries her level best to convince herself that she is the mother of the little girl to whom she gave the name Éva, ten years ago. "Éva," she had murmured to the midwife. Throughout her pregnancy she had never thought about what to call the baby, but suddenly the name Éva had come into her head at the very moment she was asked to name the child she had brought into the world.

As usual, Thérèse has to make a huge effort to turn back. From early morning she has been just driving on the autoroute that leaves the city to the north or to the west, depending on which exit one takes at the junction. As soon as Éva is at school, Thérèse takes off. She ought to do something about that job someone mentioned – the least she could do is show up for an interview. But no, Thérèse drives for hours on end, aimlessly.

Some days she takes the tram to the station. Hastily she scans the timetables for a local train on which to travel to another town, from where she will take a later train back to where she lives and where Éva will be waiting. The carriages are often virtually empty, and the stations down the line deserted, godforsaken places.

Some days Thérèse settles down on a bench on the platform, watching passengers leave and arrive, sniffing the faint smell of tar. From time to time she goes to the station café, where she keeps her white raincoat and travelling bag on the seat beside her. She doesn't read, she just sits there looking around and smoking, occasionally taking a thick spiral-bound notebook out of her bag to write something down.

On this November day she has spent all morning driving in the rain. Driving for the sake of driving, as usual, unwinding slowly in the close warmth of the car, listening to the radio: distant, disembodied voices burbling on about nothing in particular.

Rain, music, voices, speed. After a hundred kilometres Thérèse switches the radio off. The engine purrs. A faint smile flickers at her lips and a tingling sensation travels across the skin of her abdomen, her thighs, her legs, down to the ball of her foot pressing the accelerator. She knows how wild she can be. She knows she could simply take off and never go back. She toys with the idea – imagine never going back!

Ever since she and Éva came to live here she has always come back. Not always on time, but she has always come back for the little girl. Of course, if she made Éva skip school she could always put her in the back of the car and go for much longer drives, much further away. But it wouldn't be the same. She has done more than enough travelling with her daughter, more than enough driving. Now that Éva is no longer a baby, her company dulls the kick of being on the road, prevents the combined effects of speed and oblivion from taking Thérèse out of herself.

With the engine purring like a dream and the landscape turning to mauve blotting-paper, a sense of transparency comes over her at last as she rounds a final bend in the autoroute, dropping down towards the entrenched city. Thérèse is well aware that the school closed several minutes ago, that Éva is waiting all alone. Her body is still wrapped in the blissful blur of motion. If only she were distraught, filled with an anxiety that made her heart pound, then at least she would feel real. She is merely doing what she must do, in deference to a very ancient, very strict law. Her body, she, is elsewhere. She is the mist . . . The nearer the town looms the heavier the traffic grows, forcing Thérèse to slow down. This will make her even more late. Then everything is obstructed. Traffic is jammed solid. A train approaches, brightly lit, sliding parallel to the autoroute on its way to the station.

There are days too when Thérèse boards the train to Paris, on a whim. At dawn she drops Éva off at the school annexe, where the large woman in the blue smock welcomes sleepy tots from six forty-five a.m. Then she heads to the station to catch the high-speed train that leaves at seven fifty-three. She buys a ticket. Once on board, Thérèse relaxes in the musty warmth of the compartment with its mirrors for windows. The train pulls out smoothly. The glimmer of dawn, the countryside revealing itself little by little in the reflecting rectangle. The lighted windows of the houses in the countryside. The train is full of serious, respectable-looking men in dark business suits, carrying briefcases. In her seat Thérèse does not sleep. Her eyes are half-closed, she is waiting to feel truly carried away. She is waiting to become weightless and transparent, waiting to lose herself in the swaying motion of the carriage, the slight swoon of oscillation once the train glides over the skin of the earth at full tilt. Not touching the ground. A streak. That is when Thérèse leaves the cocoon of her seat to make for the buffet car.

There are men in suits standing around, shoulder to shoulder, briefcase to briefcase. Some of them are phoning with comical earnestness. Thérèse observes them. She writes something in her big notebook. There are also technicians and scientists on this early commuter train. More casual dress, too: thick sweaters, open-necked shirts, eyes glinting behind steel-framed glasses as they hold animated conversations on serious subjects.

Often there is a man who eyes her for a while before coming over and positioning himself at her side, almost touching, pretending to be absorbed in his financial newspaper and then suddenly speaking to her. Thérèse recognises the smile. The familiar smile of apprehension mixed with condescension on the clean-shaven, aftershave-reeking faces of the men travelling on trains, the men in buffet cars, department stores, parking lots. Hovering around the coffee machines at service stations, in waiting-rooms, they have this cramped smile as they prepare to strike up a conversation with a strange woman.

"Do you commute to work?"

Thérèse takes time to study the man addressing her. But she always replies, she is quite happy to talk.

"Yes . . . my job."

"Can I get you a drink?"

"All right then . . . another coffee, please."

She waves at the landscape with a smile. "Look, everything's rosy. Where *are* all these villages you see from the train? They always look so perfect, so serene, so self-sufficient . . . A church, a castle. Where are they exactly? From a car the villages never look quite as pretty as they do from the train. Haven't you noticed?"

"I don't know," the man replies. "I don't look out of the window much. Do you work in Paris?"

"All those villages . . . you can't help thinking they're just a decor put up there for the train passengers to enjoy. My job? Well, I commute, so I have to get up very early. But I'm quite lucky, I suppose."

"You reckon? I have my wife and children to consider, it's no joke having to travel such distances, but what can you do?'

"That's what I said, it's a question of luck . . ."

"Well, you don't have children, obviously. So you wouldn't understand. Do you live alone?"

Thérèse changes the subject.

"Look, the cows, in the meadows, just look at them in the rising sun, you can see how warm they are in the damp. See the steam coming from their nostrils? There's something enviable about them. I wonder what it is. Their slow pace? Their mass? All that crazy chewing of the cud, all that grass passing through their bodies and turning into milk?"

The man is taken aback, unnerved. Thérèse presses on.

"You were saying? Alone, me? No . . . it would be great to be like any of those cows, placid, solitary . . ."

Thérèse talks easily to the men who talk to her. She is friendly in a casual, detached way. She prevaricates. They think they are holding a conversation with her, but before long they have the sense that she is desperately unapproachable, and above all unsettling. Thérèse's words skim right over the men's small talk. They are travelling on a different plane, in a different direction. The men are puzzled. Their complacent smiles fade. This brief encounter in the buffet car exposes them to a disquiet they are unprepared for. They give up.

Thérèse grabs her notebook, wants to write something down, just a few lines about the cows maybe, or about that lone bull she saw a few moments ago, so sleek and strong: "Wonderful beast, oh Mighty One, I can already see all those disgusting meals you will end up as, all the steaks, racks and

[28]

roasts, all that horrible chewing and digesting to obliterate you, and you haven't a clue, oh unsuspecting creature, that you exist to order, chopped up already, dressed, jointed, cooked, turned into meals, grazing and dreaming and chewing the cud in the lush innocence of the field."

Writing this strange sentence, overlong and a little pompous, makes her feel slightly tearful and sick. Sometimes she just writes a single word, pressing so hard with her ballpoint that she gouges a hole in the page. Then she slips the notebook back into her bag.

When all the passengers have got off, when the dark suits have gone about their business, Thérèse steps down to the platform, glances left and right, takes a deep breath. She recognises the voice on the station tannoy. Sometimes it's the blonde voice, sometimes the brunette. Disembodied voices, like the ones on the radio. Young faceless females announcing departures, arrivals, delays. It is ten a.m.

Thérèse knows she must catch the 2.28 train back if she is to get home in time to pick up Éva. She has no desire to go for a stroll in Paris, not even for an hour. So she hangs around the station, passing time in the newspaper stand, browsing through the magazines, taking in the pictures. All those smiles. Those colours. Blonde girls, in the nude, as ungetatable as the voices over the loudspeaker. Glossy photographs of cars, scent bottles, mobile phones, jewellery. And more smiles and colours, women's bodies. A different world, all these beautiful, smiling creatures. She saunters off into the tumult of concourses filled with unsmiling people. A mêlée of weary bodies, shapeless, crumpled.

Thérèse takes a few coins from her purse and gives them to a prematurely aged derelict surrounded by bags spilling junk. He extends a swollen, purple hand. Then she sits down close to him, as if she in her turn is settling herself on the edge of the surging multitude.

"Not taking the train then, darling?"

"Of course I am: in a minute. I'm a bit early, that's all."

"Don't seem too keen, do you?"

"Yes yes, I'm going to take the train. I don't want to miss it. I hope there won't be a delay. I have to pick up my little girl, she's only ten . . ."

"I have a daughter myself," the man says. "A lot older than yours, though. An old bag by now, I shouldn't wonder. If I knew what had become of her and where I could find her, I wouldn't pull a face like that!"

"What face?"

"You have that spacey look, as if you more or less live in this station, like me. Airs and graces . . . none of those around here – too draughty. As for me, it's been ages since I last looked in the mirror, but with respect, darling, apart from the grime and the pimples and scabs on my skin, you and me aren't so very different."

Thérèse bolts.

So much for the stations, so much for the roads. That evening Thérèse is trapped in a monstrous traffic jam at the entrance to the city. Imprisoned in her car. A far cry from transparency, from weightlessness. Day after day, the idea of escape washes over her like water from a refreshing shower. Like blood, too, sometimes. Like blood, that is to say, blood being shed over nothing. In her spiral-bound notebook she jots down: "Lost time, lost track, lost blood".

Not far away, on the four-lane avenue probably, something has happened. She can make out the intermittent flash of blue and yellow revolving lights. Will Éva still be waiting at school? In this rain? Surely the woman in the blue smock will have told her to wait inside. Éva knows I always get there in the end . . . before long she'll be all grown up, she won't need me so much . . . then one day, she'll leave me. We've been by ourselves too much, just the two of us . . . Worse for her than for me, I expect. Too lonely to do much talking, anyway.

Hands resting on the wheel, Thérèse lets herself drift on the molten, metallic sea of traffic. On the dashboard clock she reads 5.20. The cars come to a complete standstill. Thérèse sighs. Sings to herself.

She doesn't know a soul in this town which she keeps escaping by car or by train. Some days all she does is wander around, immerse herself in the throng of department stores. She pushes the glass doors dreamily. Heads across the sparkling perfumery department, where an elaborately made-up sales assistant offers her a try of a new fragrance. Thérèse steps forward with a murmur of assent, then sniffs her wrist at length, nodding.

"The other hand, too," she asks, "and what were the names again? . . . Thank you, mademoiselle. And there too, please, between the palm and the wrist."

Thérèse moves away without buying anything. Roaming department stores, like riding trains, gives her a pleasantly light, wadded feeling in the head. Éva is at school. Time seems limitless. She can see her reflection in the mirrors, but she isn't interested in her looks. The idea of seducing, the very idea of being fancied doesn't enter her mind. She threads her way discreetly between things and bodies. There she is, standing still on an escalator taking her to the next floor. To her the atmosphere is becalmed, the hubbub of human voices no more than a capsule of silence enclosing her.

Passing to the lingerie section, she strolls between banks of foaming lace and nylon, pausing now and then to be lapped by little waves of the softest pink, white, cream, red, black. She fingers a bra, selects a slip at random, scrunches it up in her hand as if it were a silken bird that she could either spare or crush to death. Her thoughts stray briefly to all those real stomachs belonging to real women which will soon be straining against these brand-new fabrics. Buttocks, breasts, thighs, stomachs, all will be concealed – or revealed, as the case may be – by the pristine underwear waiting on the display counters. This is the kind of fleeting impression that Thérèse writes down in her spiral-bound notebook.

Different clothes for different people. She imagines bodies coming from all directions . . . "They come from the four corners of the future to dress the meat, to carve the cattle into a hundred portions and eat them. The bodies come from the future to dress up in all the beautiful new clothes and pull them out of shape, to try on the snow-white underwear for size and make it shop-soiled. It's sad and of no importance." Having written this down, Thérèse copies out the last words in capital letters that are too big for the small-squared writing paper: "SAD AND OF NO IMPORTANCE".

If there is still enough time before she has to collect Éva from school, Thérèse moves on to the ladies' fashions to try on some dresses. Sometimes she dawdles over her choice, other times she grabs things at random which she wouldn't dream of buying. She shuts the curtain of the changing cubicle, sheds her clothes and puts on one outfit after another, outfits that would suit an older woman, evening gowns, sexy frocks, clinging, low-cut at the back, the shoulders, the chest, unbecoming woollen dressing gowns, ridiculous, loud, floral ensembles, pretty, floaty dresses.

Thérèse takes her time in the cubicle, but rarely glances in the mirror. Her reflection is of no interest to her. All she wants is to lose herself in the successive garments, which she discards in a heap on the floor when she is done. She pays no attention to how she looks in them. She sits down on the bench behind the closed curtain and shuts her eyes, trying among the welter of new dresses to feel some emotion. She waits and listens. The world brushes so close that she can feel it on her skin, through all manner of fabrics. She sniffs at her over-scented wrists again. Inhales. Sighs. Smiles. In her notebooks she writes "feels all right, not being anyone . . . a non-person".

Then comes the moment, after all that leisurely browsing, that she must tear herself away or she will be late. Éva, it's always Éva and the strict times kept by schools and janitors. Her daughter Éva! She even wrote "Éva is my child" several times over in her notebook, as though to convince herself of this fact. And also, boxed in, the words "Éva is all I have in the whole world". Indeed, most of the time Thérèse does succeed in being a mother of sorts. She does what she can for her daughter. She concentrates, makes an effort to remember all Éva's needs. And the years go by. When Éva was still a baby, acting like a proper mother was easier, in a way. She has turned into a pretty little girl, growing fast. Pretty soon, fortunately, she'll be old enough to manage on her own now and then. And all the while Thérèse fights the poisonous desire not to go back . . .

Traffic grinds to a halt on the bridge, then crawls in the downpour along the embankment. Her progress to her daughter's school is excruciatingly slow. Nearly two hours late! On an impulse she abandons her car to walk the rest of the way in the freezing rain. She can't believe how deserted the street looks, plunged in a dim silence as though everyone who lived there has suddenly been evicted. The school gate is shut tight behind curtains of rain. When someone turns up at last to let her in it is not the big woman who has so often seen her arrive late and who keeps an eye on Éva for her; it is a young blonde woman she has never seen before. The sense of unreality intensifies.

The young woman asks Thérèse cheerfully which child she has come to collect.

"But you're not . . . What about the lady who works here normally?"

"I'm standing in for her today."

Thérèse has already seen that Éva is not among the small gathering of tired-looking children reading and playing in the overheated room.

"Blanchot, I'm Thérèse Blanchot. I was held up . . . Éva? Didn't she wait for me here, out of the rain? Haven't you seen her?"

A little girl comes forward, proclaiming, "Éva went home. She was waiting in the rain. I saw her. And then she ran off."

Thérèse crosses the courtyard in the rain just as Éva did a while back. The gate squeaks. The walls loom darkly. The cobbles are slick and slippery underfoot. Thérèse sets off again in the direction of their flat. She knows her daughter won't be able to find her way home on her own. Too many crossroads, too many streets that look the same.

Thérèse tells herself that by now Éva must have got well and truly lost in this city surrounded by mountains, snow and night. No need to hurry, then. She is merely returning to her temporary home in a nondescript neighbourhood, soaked to the skin, streaked red, yellow and blue by the lambent city lights, numbed by the blare of horns, sirens, engines. When she finally arrives there are two uniformed policemen waiting on her doorstep: "Madame Blanchot?"

The Wait

RESUSCITATION, INTENSIVE CARE, TRAUMATOLOGY. Departmental treasure hunt. Sixth floor, seventh, heavy doors parting quietly to let stretcher trolleys through. As no-one stops him, no-one says, "Monsieur? Are you looking for someone? Monsieur! It's not visiting time yet," Vollard presses on through the pristine dreamscape with the white smell of disinfectant and ether. A blinding, over-heated maze. Confusing signs. TRAUMATOLOGY. And then, finally: RESUSCITATION.

All along the endless corridors the doors are open, offering glimpses of prostrate bodies, some of them half-naked. Something tells you they are not really asleep. The eyes staring ahead are not fully awake either, nor are the lids in the sallow faces lowered in sleep. There is a sense of narcotics at work, dulling the pain and clearing the decks for wholesale apathy, the limp apathy of wounded, amputated bodies being nursed, cosseted, stitched up, repaired, bandaged. Like a coma or semi-sleep. Bodies waiting for what will happen next, or for the end.

Vollard walks as unobtrusively as possible, trying not to let his shoes squeak on the tiles. Everything seems frozen in time, under the sway of gleaming appliances. On his way to the very last room, where he is convinced she must be, he goes past a spacious glassed-in ward bustling with white coats, but no-one seems to notice the hulking stranger in his torn and mud-stained clothes.

The last door in the corridor is open, but the bed is empty, the white sheets barely rumpled. Vollard freezes on the threshold. Is this what he has come all this way for? The hammer blow of this appalling void? Then he notices the slight figure of a woman at the window, hugging herself as if she is cold. A young woman lost in blank contemplation of high-rise buildings, desolate concrete. No mountains.

It is their first encounter: Vollard's mass filling the doorway, Thérèse's silhouette diffracting into the greyness outside, and between them a gulf of silence filled with the absence of the child.

Vollard, who was trying not to make a sound, breathes again, deeply and audibly. When he exhales it is a long, wheezing sigh, as though an idiotic hope is ebbing endlessly away. Thérèse turns, slowly. She too is drained.

"You're not the doctor, are you?" she asks in a small voice.

Vollard shakes his head.

"This is the room of the little girl . . . "

"She's my daughter, Éva."

"It was me driving, yesterday, on the avenue . . . saw her too late . . . I need to know."

"They've taken her back to the operating theatre. Just now I thought she'd died. After the first operation she

[37]

looked so pale, sort of transparent. They took her away again. It was a haemorrhage, and it wouldn't stop. They told me they were doing everything they could, but . . ."

"Please understand, I had to find out. I had to see her. I've been looking for . . . When will they know?"

Thérèse seems not to notice Vollard's bedraggled appearance, the torn clothing, the dried blood.

"All we can do is wait. I'm glad you came. The police told me there was nothing you could do to avoid her, that she was in a complete panic."

"Nothing I could do? I could have avoided her. I should have. What's the point of living to my age if you can't even avoid such a terrible thing? After the accident, when they told me to go, I just drove around for a long time. How long has she been in the operating theatre?"

"Since the middle of the night. She was in a very bad way. They've started all over again. The skull, of course. And organs ruptured. She hasn't regained consciousness."

Vollard catches the tiny creaking of wheels in the corridor. He puts his head round the door, but at the far end of the corridor a hospital bed is disappearing around a corner. A vague shape covered by a white sheet. Thérèse resumes staring out of the window.

Vollard can't stop himself moving, stretching, reaching out to the walls, for the ceiling, pacing like a caged beast. He suppresses the urge to smash his fist down on the bedside table. He knows just how it would shatter to pieces, crassly, making a lot of noise, so he concentrates on splaying his fingers instead of clenching his fists. He is breathing heavily, muttering to himself.

"I was late," Thérèse begins. "I can't seem to manage to get to her school on time. That was what I should have been able to avoid. She wasn't looking where she was going, she was running. I was thinking of Éva, all alone like that, but I didn't think she'd panic. I didn't think . . . I never do, when it's important. I'm all she's got, you know. But I never thought that anything like this could happen."

Vollard hears none of this. "They are keeping her a very long time . . . I'm going to see the nurses. It's suffocating in here. There must be a doctor somewhere."

"No, please, stay and wait with me. I feel as if I don't ever want to know. I would rather they never told me anything more, never came back. I can stay right here, by the window. If you hadn't turned up, I think I would have fallen asleep on my feet. I wish I could crumble to dust, float away like the snowflakes outside. Not think of anything any more."

"But surely you think of your child. About what they're doing with her, right now!"

"Yes, I do think about her. When I make myself think. Which can get to be too much at times. I think how I love her. Loved her ever since I first laid eyes on her. I said 'Éva', just like that, straight away. When it came down to it, I knew everything would be fine, even without a father. But when I first got pregnant I couldn't believe I'd have a child at the end of it, and that the child would belong to me. I wasn't at all fat. I just did nothing until she was actually born,

[39]

that's how unconvinced I was. I was terribly lonely. Only a woman alone with a baby could understand."

"But once you had the little girl? The fragile body . . . the wide-eyed look at things—"

"You don't understand at all, do you? Having a child just makes loneliness so much harder to bear. It's not that it turns you into an animal, it turns you into a thing. Every morning, every night I'd tell myself you're a mummy now, you've got to do this, you've got to do that, all the things proper mummies do . . . "

"And did you?"

"Yes, pretty much. Éva always got what she needed, more or less. But there was this other voice—"

"What voice?"

"The voice saying 'Run away, Thérèse, run away!'"

"Run away?"

"Yes, that's what I remember, those two words."

"Which was more important, the flight or the salvation?"

"What are you getting at? You seem to like complicating everything. Run away, do a runner, that's all! All I ever want, doesn't matter where I am, is to get away, even here, even now. When Éva was little I used to take her with me everywhere. We were on the move a lot of the time, did a lot of travelling, of getting away. I used to wrap her up nice and warm, lay her in her Moses basket on the back seat and off we'd go. I always managed to keep her with me each time I found a job. Refused to let her out of my sight. Wasn't having it."

"Why not?"

"I don't know, or rather yes, I do know."

"You'd have forgotten her?"

"Yes. Not abandoned: forgotten. After work I'd have gone wandering off around town. On my own. Looking at everything. Looking at people, things, nothing special. Wanting to be alone. Wanting to talk, didn't matter who to. Following people at random."

"Random men, you mean?"

"Sometimes, I suppose. On account of some trifling thing, some sign I can see hovering around a person's body, or their face, something they're completely unaware of. I can see things. Dead childhoods. Or messed-up lives so humdrum it makes you want to cry. Nice-looking types, well-dressed, you know, the kind of men who reckon they've done rather well for themselves, whereas their lives are more dismal than mine. I see the shabbiness. And the fear, too. It has an effect on me. That's how I was given Éva. There was a gesture, a tone of voice that moved me, and then, very quickly, there was a phantom father."

"This heat is unbearable. I stink. I spent half the night on the mountain, walking. I fell. I'm filthy."

"You're hurt. Are you in pain?"

"I'm aching just about all over, but that'll pass."

"I can smell earth and forest on your clothes. Sweat, too. I noticed your bruises when you came in, and your torn jacket, and the blood. But I also saw your strength."

"My strength?"

"Vulnerability, then. Not that much difference between them as far as I can see. I'm not very good at saying what I think . . ."

Vollard veers round to the washbasin and turns the cold tap on full. The mirror is too low for him, but stooping as he cups his hands he can see his reflection. What Vollard sees is a mass of pepper-and-salt and ginger hair plastered on a forehead that has been bleeding heavily; green eyes with crow's feet and dark rings of fatigue; his cheeks likewise bearded in pepper-and-salt and russet with bits of twig and dried mud. This shaggy, filthy individual is him, and he is appalled. How could this young woman have been talking to such a monster? How could she just go ahead and tell her life story to the man who may have killed her daughter? Who on earth can this strange young woman be?

He splashes cold water on his cheeks, eyes, forehead. He pushes back his wet hair, grimaces, dabs and cleans the cut on his face, rakes his thick fingers through his beard, snorts the water away, straightens himself up, and opens his eyes to find the hospital room swarming with white-coated nurses. Vollard has to stand back against the wall to let the metal trolley pass.

It is a type of wheeled stretcher, carrying a burden so slight as to seem non-existent. A small blurry outline buried under a sheet and hooked up to machines with clear plastic bags of intravenous fluids. It can't be the child, merely what is left of her. There is no forehead, no hair to be seen, only bandages. No cheeks, no nose, only an oxygen mask and a head clamp.

No arms, only two waxen limbs dotted with needles connected to tubes.

Vollard remains glued to the wall. Thérèse waits by the window. Nurses bustle about. Gently they slide the small body from the trolley to the bed with the shiny bars, then they attach appliances that require regulating with minute and very grave precision. They hook up the intravenous drip. Luminous digital displays and bleeping instruments surround the body, which is so tiny that Vollard can barely distinguish the lowered eyelids in the space above the oxygen mask and below the bandages.

More staff, this time in green, crowd into the already teeming room. The senior consultant, hairy forearms, gold-rimmed spectacles, glances from Vollard to Thérèse and back. As Vollard is the only one to stir, it is to him that he decides to address his little speech.

"She will be all right. She will pull through. We've dealt with the haemorrhage. The legs and the shoulder, they'll be all right. As for the head, that's another matter. We will have to keep a close eye on her. It won't be until she regains consciousness that we will know more. We'll have to wait and see."

"Wait for what? See what?" cries Thérèse. "That's horrible, how can I wait?"

"It's too early to say," the doctor says. "There's no way of knowing yet. The impact to her skull was extremely violent."

"But she'll wake up, won't she? Come to?" Vollard asks.

[43]

"Coma is a most mysterious thing. We have done all we possibly can."

One by one the white and green medics file out of the room, until only a nurse with pale blue eyes in a round face is left behind, bent over the oxygen mask. She appears to be smiling at the desperately closed eyes. She touches the child's forehead fleetingly. Thérèse hovers in the background, wary of getting close to the machines and tubes. Then Vollard notices Éva's dark eyebrows, arched in an expression of surprise and exhaustion, utterly detached from the swaddle of bed sheets and flicker of fluorescent digits. In his mind he sees the wide-eyed look again. In slow motion, the interminable fraction of a second when the little girl's eyes were locked with his own. Éva at the jaws of death, Vollard powerless to save her.

The day grinds on. Vollard comes and goes, slumps massively on to a chair, rises again, and grumbles. Thérèse remains lost in contemplation of the snow. Two or three times she says she should get some fresh air, and each time Vollard wonders whether she intends to come back.

The nurse with the pale blue eyes is present nearly all the time, and it seems to Vollard, observing her, that the way she smiles at the unconscious child, the way she caresses the little alabaster hands, are part of a miracle drug of which she alone knows the formula.

"It's important to keep talking to this little girl," she says to this peculiar couple, "isn't it, Éva? Because you can hear us, can't you? Because you are going to hear us, Éva."

She is the first to call the child by her Christian name.

As the afternoon draws to a close, Vollard says it is time he went home, but that he will be back if he may. It means a lot to him. Thérèse seems very distant. Impatient and defeated at the same time.

"I don't think I can stay much longer either. Talk to her? What on earth can I talk about? Look, she's not even moving. My being here isn't doing any good. I've got to—"

"Escape?"

Vollard gives an exasperated shrug, breathing hard through his nose. Paying no further mind to Thérèse, he walks away with a heavy tread. Shaggy, smelling of dog, ground down with exhaustion, with sleeplessness, he moves slowly down the corridors. Outside, even the icy air fails to rouse him. The snow is no longer falling, and what had settled is now rapidly turning into slush. Bookseller Vollard goes in search of his van, which, miraculously, he finds. He gets in, shuts the door, slumps back and falls instantly asleep. Wedged in between seat and wheel. Head lolling. The accident happened twenty-four hours ago. Landscape turned upside down. Time burst. It is no longer the same town. It will not be the same life. Banal and sticky, the accident has suckered itself like an octopus on to everything.

In his sleep Vollard has gradually sagged sideways over the passenger seat, the "death seat". His thighs are still wedged under the wheel, but his head is propped against the right-hand door with the handle pressing into his bearded cheek.

[45]

Bolstering his big shoulders and back are dozens of spilled novels: *Divine Comedy, Metamorphoses, Nausea, La Vie courante, The Red and the Black* . . .

One glimpse of a cover, plain or illustrated, and Vollard can place it instantaneously: publisher, approximate date of publication, series, title, author, but presently his exceptional memory overloads his mind with long quotes, passages of varying lengths which he has retained since he first read the work. Indeed, Vollard will recognise any book, even if read a very long time ago, by the crystalline murmur starting up in his head, burbling, streaming, brimming over and sometimes even setting his lips in silent motion.

Often, he can visualise the exact printed text lodged at the back of his mind. An amazing memory. Memory for nothing but words of bookseller Vollard who harbours, in the depths of his frame, the meat of millions of words once ingested, chewed, rechewed, ruminated, still in pristine condition, in a never-tiring cycle of delight. A scene in a novel comes back to him in every detail, complete with the corresponding page layout, typeface, smell of glue and paper, and even the blank spaces, the punctuation, the word-break at the end of a line, with part of it hanging on by a hyphen and the balance forlornly embarking on the next line.

After an hour of stupor, Vollard wakes with a jolt, a crumpled page sticking to his lips.

"And I went unto the angel, and said unto him, Give me the little book. And he said unto me, Take it, and eat it up: and it shall make thy belly bitter, but it shall be in thy mouth sweet as honey.

And I took the little book out of the angel's hand, and ate it up: and it was in my mouth sweet as honey: and as soon as I had eaten it, my belly was bitter."

Vollard heaves himself into an upright position, setting off another landslide of books in the half-light. His belly is filled with bitterness, but so is his mouth. He wants to stretch his body, extricate himself, understand what has happened. His view through the windscreen is blocked by a thick rectangle of snow. He inhales loudly. His joints crack as he straightens his arms, clenching and unclenching his fists. He places his hands on the wheel, grips it with all his might.

Then it all comes back to him: the speed, the rain, the little girl in red he is hurtling down upon, the look in her eyes, the crash, the noise. Instinctively, he slams on the brake pedal, takes hold of the wheel, wrenches it towards him. He sits, paralysed, open-mouthed, thinking that he can hear the echo of his own scream in the mountains. His recollection of the past twenty-four hours is like an amputated hand, a giant's hand, thick and frozen, flung into his face, triggering another memory: *"The horror, the horror . . . "* Just these words: *"The horror."*

He opens the door, steps out into the slush and with great pain stretches to his full height. He decides against clearing the snow off the windscreen; he will not start the engine and drive away. He can only walk. He will walk at a brisk pace, hands thrust deep into his pockets.

Arriving in the city centre at last, Vollard tramps on in the direction of the shadowy embankments and the old

[47]

neighbourhoods. Turning abruptly into a deserted square, he finds himself in front of his own shop with the sign saying THE VERB TO BE – BOOKS, NEW AND SECOND-HAND. Framed in the sober façade, the window looks like an illuminated fish tank in the night, with paper fish suspended behind the wall of glass. Peering through the glazed door with its ridged handle like the spine of a leather-bound book, he can make out the figure of Madame Pélagie, sere, nimble, dressed in black. Loyal factotum, efficient, ageless.

He observes her reaching for a book on a high shelf, turning swiftly to write something down, busying herself with other books while a last-minute customer – the one Vollard had nicknamed "Big-mouth Boncassa", the ever-present Boncassa hunched over some old tome – lifts his head to break into one of his usual tirades on the imminent demise of literature and the dearth of proper writers and proper books. From the street Vollard can only see Boncassa's gesticulations, but he can guess each turn in the peroration, up to and including the latest news about the secret masterpiece this patron claims to have been labouring over each night since he was a boy.

Madame Pélagie. Boncassa. A grey-haired, middle-aged pair. Ethereal presences. Vollard remains motionless watching the little scene that is more surprisingly familiar than ever.

The Verb To Be

"The Verb To Be" was the name of an old bookshop. A murky place, due not to a lack of lighting but to all the nooks and crannies. A deep space with dark, worn floorboards and secluded niches. Books everywhere, spread on tables and upright in rows, thousands of silent observers on wooden shelves.

An ongoing battle between dust and the printed word at "The Verb To Be", cardboard boxes overflowing with books, piles of volumes threatening to topple. Anarchy reigning supreme. Grandiose anarchy. A profusion of genres and titles. A joyous alchemy. It was here that people could drop by any day to procure their reading matter, highbrow or popular, arcane or classic, in exchange for a modest sum.

The kind of retreat that future generations will be hard put to imagine because nothing like it will exist any more, because this blend of painstaking order and clutter, of reverence for books and stacking them in promiscuous heaps, will have gone up in smoke. Business on a small scale. Discreet custom, but a basic necessity. A bastion of text and print. Anodyne, but explosive all the same. Sleek stocks of flares, capable equally of lighting up life's small details and illuminating vast swathes of existence. As the Chinese sage said: "*The exquisite delight of discovering a sea of stories that one has not yet perused. Or acquiring the second volume of a work after falling in love with the first."*

Over the display counters hung several shaded lamps diffusing a soft glow, in which thirsty readers could stoop for a private sip of the refreshments on offer. Champagne, infernal elixirs, heady wines, liqueurs, plain red and pure water. The dimness at the far end of the bookshop always took some getting used to, but on some mornings the sun poured in so generously through the glazed door that it was impossible to resist going over there and opening a book in broad daylight, letting it warm the pages and show up the grain of the paper so that the whiteness would stretch out like a desert of signs. Leisure, light, literature: true happiness!

At the turn of the twenty-first century it was scornfully prophesied that places like this were on the way out. So much for the local bookshop! Done for, that type of trade . . . It was paper they held in contempt, and ink. The ink used for writing as well as for printing: messy, antiquated practices. But they also disdained the little repositories of thoughts, visions, words unfurling page after page while remaining singularly compact, self-contained, just right for slipping into your pocket, taking on a journey and opening never mind where, never mind when. To be read. Devoured. Leafed through. No electricity, no screens. "Guess where I'm reading the *Treatise on the Improvement of Understanding,* or the *Stanzas* of Agrippa d'Aubigné!" On a train. In the cleft of a rock at the seaside. In bed. In a crowd.

On the lavatory. Lying in a bubble bath. In the beam of a head torch at the foot of a sand dune, in the wind.

There is a warmth about all those books: bought in bookshops, treasured, given away as presents, abandoned to their own recondite fates. Torn, yellowed, forgotten, re-discovered. Reams of great texts . . . *"Habent sua fata libelli."*

Book stories. Vollard the bookseller liked telling the story of the man who was held hostage for years by a group of politico-religious fanatics in the Middle East and who, by the most extraordinary stroke of luck, discovered a copy of *War and Peace* volume II hidden in a corner of his squalid cell. Mangled and mildewed, but translated into his own language. A book in no better shape than he was. From then on something changed for him. Everything changed. An immense solace came to him from the scores of pages spilling from between the covers, and his taste for life was restored.

Vollard also told the story of the woman condemned to total darkness in a Soviet jail, who kept in her head a Shakespeare play she had committed to memory as a girl. Sightless, in the solitary confinement that induces madness, she recited *King Lear* to herself in English, from start to finish. A pinpoint of light gathered in her gloom. She could see the book, she could see the words. So she read, turning the pages in her mind's eye. She saw it so clearly, the book she had bought in a little shop when she was a student, that she began to translate it into Russian, in the dark, just for her, no other reason, just a way of keeping the embers of humanity alive in the face of all oppression. She turned the pages of her old student's copy in the course of an extremely vivid hallucination. Trawling her memory for the exact word, the cadence, the cohesion, she passed her time translating, with neither ink nor paper, as she waited for death.

Étienne Vollard spent most of his time sitting in the back, a giant spider in the centre of his web. From the old flat where he lived immediately above "The Verb To Be" he came down daily to sell his books. Every day up until the accident, that is, Vollard the bookseller came down the stairs to keep vigil by the sickbed of Literature. Her breathing was laboured. She was feverish. But still breathing.

For a long time he had known how to read the signs and welcome new developments, but nowadays, he said, things do not change the way they used to, there is just a parody of change that changes nothing. Even so, he never gave up mining the avalanches of textual merchandise, the plethora of fly-by-nights paradoxically named "books", the jostling crowd of self-proclaimed writers, in the hope of extracting a gem. In the meantime his memory, like his body, expanded.

That evening, on the small deserted square, facing the lighted shop window, Vollard could not bring himself to step inside. He was in no state to be seen, bespattered and dejected, but especially he was in no state to account for himself. He could not just push the door open, stride down the aisle and declare to a frowning Madame Pélagie, or to Boncassa who didn't give a fig about anything unless it was happening in a book: "You know what? Yesterday on the

avenue, at five in the afternoon, I ran down a child!"
Unthinkable. So he let himself into the unlit entryway that
led up to his flat.

PART II

First Acquaintance

I know very little of the life of Étienne Vollard. There are vast blanks. Swathes of uncertainties. To speak of this man I have had to resort to an old novelistic ritual, which is causing me qualms. Here I am, embarked on my story, and it's a bit like waking up on the bridge of a phantom tub in high seas, buffeted, helmless, caught in crosscurrents. Between anxiety and elation.

The fact is that Vollard's story is clamped on my brain, talons and suckers, tooth and nail. I see him before me – before the accident, of course – surrounded by books, in an old part of the town where I had recently been posted. But equally as a schoolboy flitting across my own youth, and then again some years later, as a young man. And in sleepless vigils I distinctly hear the terrible scream that Vollard let out that night on the Chartreuse mountain.

There is this recurring nightmare: I am in a vehicle I cannot control, my legs are too short to reach the pedals, there is no-one with me and I am on the point of smashing into a body that is vulnerability itself. Fragile face, wide terrified eyes.

It also happens that I dream of those thousands upon thousands of books among which Vollard lived, all those texts ingrained in his astonishing memory since childhood.

Even today, opening one of my own books at random, I find myself labouring over passages which I know Vollard would be capable of quoting verbatim, articulating each phrase with spirit or else letting the words roll off the tongue more or less mindless of their meaning, in a sort of fluidity of sound.

> *"I am as a cat burnt alive*
> *Crushed by the wheel of a big truck*
> *Strung up in a fig tree by boys*
> *But still with at least six of its seven lives to go,*
> *Like a snake reduced to a bloody pulp, a half-eaten eel . . ."*

Browsing among my books for the umpteenth time, it occurs to me that, all things considered, I wouldn't mind being a bookseller myself: spending the greater part of my time in the company of writers, discovering them, getting people to read them, promoting their sales, soliciting for them, implicating myself in their deals with the reading public. A dealer in literary drugs. A fin-de-siècle bookseller.

How many people in the not too distant future will be left who understand what bookshops and booksellers used to mean to people like me? The difference it made to a town or city if there were such places one could go into in the hope of some revelation? Who will recall the tranquil manner in which one penetrated those warrens redolent of paper and print? The way of tilting the head to decipher one title after another, scan the names of authors familiar or unknown, glean clues from the pale covers? *"The only true reader is the thoughtful reader."* Who will recall the way of placing the index finger at the top of the spine to tip the volume backwards, then drawing it out, opening it, leafing through it, reading the blurb. Standing amid the riffle of pages, encountering a few words that appear to be addressed directly to oneself. The unhoped-for reassurance in black and white. An all-embracing, intimate acquaintance. Soundless music.

In the depths of the shop the proprietor keeps himself aloof, which is as it should be, since it is he who has made the encounter possible, who has set out the books in a certain way, who has presented them, brought them together. He is lord and master of the store, the leader of readers, the shepherd of words ever mindful of the likes and dislikes of his customers. It is often he who first discovers a great work, and he who finds the words to talk of words, who states the price – by definition risible – of what he knows to be invaluable.

Is that why Étienne Vollard keeps edging into my consciousness? Is it the bookseller in him or the dangerous driver? The bookseller as killer? Or is it his freakish power of recall? The walking library he has been all his life? The man bowed by malaise and misfortune? It is not that I resemble him. I am neither tall nor hefty, neither solitary nor mnemonically gifted, and I don't run over children except in my nightmares. My memory is not particularly good at all, which is why I have to keep going back to the books I have read to look things up. Besides, my life is largely uneventful and my intellect plodding.

I met Vollard a very long time ago. Our paths crossed when we were boys. Some years later I saw him again, very briefly, but it was only recently that I stepped into his bookshop. It was a few months before the accident with the little girl. He didn't realise who I was. I did not approach him, I was just another customer. He kept to himself behind a large grey table littered with books and papers. I saw him stuff notes and cheques into a cigar box. We did not speak to each other. Right now, Vollard's story demands to enter the world, like a monstrous, premature foetus. Everything in me is tensing in order to push it out. And everything in me is holding it in.

The first time I saw him was in class. Not from a front-row vantage point, for I was lost among forty boys aged thirteen and fourteen packed in a classroom at the oldest lycée in Lyon. It was a morning in autumn, a few weeks after the beginning of term. I was feeling drowsy and slightly sick, and for all the explanations of the maths teacher, tall and thin with a shiny pate and pockets bulging with chalks in every colour, I had dropped off in the close warmth, which, coming after the biting cold of the street, enabled me to prolong a while my night's rest.

Without warning the door opens. Forty boys rise to their feet in a din of scraping chairs. The headmaster comes in, snowy moustache and navy-blue pinstripe, shakes hands with the teacher, faces the class and announces that there will be forty-one of us from now on, as he is presenting a new colleague. The boy looks away. His arms hang awkwardly by his sides. He is already taller than the principal, stouter, too.

Tightly cribbed in a thick black velvet jacket. Short trousers, crumpled socks. Puffy cheeks, dark circles under the eyes. Long thick thighs, huge ruddy knees, a vast forehead, and then that brazier on his head, that shock of flaming red hair, not ginger, no hint of yellow.

"Make room for Monsieur Vollard," the principal intones. More scraping of chairs, and the next moment he is in our midst, massive, striking. The idea takes hold that the new boy being dumped on us for some strange reason is not all there, or at any rate definitely backward. He looks much older than us. The lesson resumes, but everyone sneaks looks at the newcomer listening attentively to the teacher with the hands of many colours. He seems to take up as much space as two or three pupils. His eyes are very black and glinting, and no-one wants to meet them.

When the teacher inquires whether he is able to follow the lesson he nods, muttering "Yes." Why is it that, although the new boy hasn't said or done anything yet, his reply unleashes such hilarity?

"At the school you were before, Monsieur Vollard, did you do maths?"

"Yes."

Another burst of laughter. Wide awake now, I hoot along with the others. The whole class senses that there is sport to be had with this lumbering redhead. There is a menacing edge to our guffaws, no doubt to mask an inadmissible fear. Red hair. The size of his limbs, his hands. A pack of boys scenting opportunities for cruelty.

[61]

During the first break-time he was left alone. A lone figure slumped against the wall of the playground, fumbling in his jacket pockets, staring at his shoes. During the second break the new boy was jostled, remarks were made about his weight and especially his hair. The third day he was bumped into a few times as though to test how the hulking mass would react. People pushed him from behind and ran away. But Vollard did not react, aside from sketching weary gestures with his large arms, or shaking his head disconsolately. It was not long before we discovered that his pockets were stuffed with books. Surreptitious hands would slip in and deftly snatch a mysterious volume. Only then did he respond, lungeing forward to retrieve his property. His fury struck us as comic rather than frightening. We set upon him to make him run. He didn't hit back at his assailants, all he cared about was his book. Each time he came near, the book was hurled to the other end of the playground. Vollard spun round. He kept lurching after his book like a bull obsessed by a red cape. This was the first of a spate of spectacular corridas. And the precious book was ripped apart.

Whatever he did was met with roars of laughter and applause, with loud olés. He kept his temper, did not lash out, indeed he never even raised his huge fists; all he wished, when we drifted into other games, was to be left in peace so he could lean against the wall of the playground with his nose buried in a book.

His appearance was not the only reason for our cruelty. Vollard was steeped in loneliness, so it seemed. He was lonely all over, in his gloomy eyes, in every gesture, and even in his smile, for he did smile at us from time to time, not sadly or submissively, but luminously. He often held his bottom lip in a slight pout, mouth ajar, and without warning a huge smile would light up his face. What did he see? He was not smiling at us, but at something that was way over our heads. It was a lonely smile. He seemed to have knowledge of a secret, fleeting happiness from which ordinary, brutish boys like us were excluded, and this idea increased our rage tenfold. One of the things people said about him was that he was an orphan. Where did he come from? What had his life been like, what had he experienced that we couldn't begin to imagine? After school he ducked into narrow side streets where we did not dare follow him. He was said to be living with a foster family.

In class he was not an outstanding pupil, he rushed his homework, was careless with his exercise books. One day, however, everyone had to concede that Étienne Vollard's memory was phenomenal. Yet another occasion for savage laughter. Everything that had to be memorised for home-work Vollard could reel off word perfect. First in elocution, needless to say: he knew all the poems in our French book by heart. He could have been top of the class in history, as in all other subjects, for he was able to retain the content of our textbooks with disconcerting ease and down to the last comma, but when required to write he just scribbled a couple of sentences, the briefest of commentaries, before handing it in.

It was when he was called to the dais, flaming red hair in front of the blackboard, that he was at his most spectacular. He loomed over us, an absurd tower asking to be toppled.

"Now, to the blackboard" . . . the teacher said. "Let's see . . . You, Vollard!"

At which the whole classroom burst out laughing. It was an automatic reflex: the mere utterance of his name was enough to make everyone snigger. Vollard–Tub-of-Lard. And I didn't hold back either. On one occasion I even joined in the destruction of one of his books, after I had read out a few phrases here and there without understanding a word.

"Come along, Vollard, hurry up and try not to bump into the furniture on your way."

The boys sitting behind him jammed their heels against Vollard's chair to keep him to his desk as long as possible. Patiently, he extricated himself. Pencil cases and rulers clattered to the floor as he made his way to the dais, but as soon as the teacher motioned him to relate the passage to be mastered, an expectant hush took hold. We knew the words would pour from his lips exactly as in the printed text. The big, bookish boy inspired a hateful respect in us, a grudging admiration. The better his performance, the more savagely we would treat him during the break.

Vollard would let himself be propelled to a secluded part of the playground, at the back of the big plane trees or near the urinals. We would form a circle round him, forcing him to recite anything, didn't matter what. Our demands were perverse. One of us, finger painstakingly following the lines of a library book, checked to make sure our victim made no mistake. Vollard did his thing. The least hesitation, the slightest inaccuracy earned him a slap with the ruler on his thick knees or a jab in his rump with a pair of compasses. We treated him like a circus animal, whereas he was a mental phenomenon, an effortless prodigy of nature.

We soon tired of this game, but that did not mean to say we let him be.

"Come on! Let's play cops-and-Vollard!"

The circle opened up. After more prodding and shoving Vollard broke into a slow, heavy trot round the yard. He was the sole robber, and all of the rest of us were the cops. We hounded our red-haired quarry until he was winded, exhausted, scarlet-faced.

Every time he slackened his pace or stopped, we pummelled him to run some more. When he slumped against one of the plane trees, a hail of kicks to his ribs and thighs ensued. We twisted his ears, pulled his hair out by the handful. Once we even rubbed his nose on the ground in the yard. He bled, but did not complain. When the bell rang, we swiftly helped him to his feet. Ten or twelve of us hoisted him upright, brushed him down, pulled up his socks, made him wipe his nose on his sleeve. We hustled him to the classroom, our very own oversized, living toy. An apparently inoffensive hulk.

To find some peace during break-times, or between midday and two p.m. (he did not come to the canteen, as he either skipped lunch altogether or just nibbled a crust of

[65]

bread), Vollard often holed up in an empty classroom. He liked reading on his feet. Head bowed, absorbed and absorbing, the absolute reader. One day he was standing by a wide-open window with the sun on his cheeks and on the book in his hands, when five boys stole into the room. Vollard's back was turned.

His isolation was horrific, but there was also a strange sense of enjoyment, an unmistakable enjoyment which his classmates could not abide. He was so engrossed in his reading that he did not hear the soft squeak of the door, nor the creak of the old floorboards. He did not feel the air stirring and did not notice the smell of adolescent sweat. Stealthy approach. Stifled laughter.

Suddenly the five pounced on Vollard. For all his bulk and impressive size, they seized him by the seat of his pants, hoisted him up and heaved him out of the window. A bunch of other boys hovered in the doorway, cheering them on and applauding their vileness as if it were an achievement. The classroom Vollard had been reading in was on the ground floor, so it was only a metre or so that he fell, but that did not make their intent any the less barbaric. Vollard landed heavily on the paving bricks, which must have been very painful. His book had slipped from his grasp during the ambush. Some boys retrieved it and hurled it in his face. The pages fluttered helplessly in the sun. Too sluggish, too indecisive, I hadn't had time to grab the book and hide it about my person so I could read it when I got home – no doubt with very mixed feelings. Because I was there, of course . . . a bystander, at least

I hope that's all I was, but present none the less. And then the baying pack poured into the playground to encircle Vollard, get him to his feet and dust him off, slapping him hard on the shoulders all the while.

Shameful, confusing memories of my earliest encounter with Étienne Vollard. Mingling most discreetly, most cravenly, with the persecutors, I was filled with fascination for the new boy, not that I would admit it even to myself, let alone to my classmates. Not wanting to be different, I couldn't risk letting on how I longed to know what was in those recondite books.

The time I stole several crumpled pages from Vollard and stuffed them down my trousers, my heart leapt into my throat. Back in class, installed in an anonymous third row, I quaked at the idea of being labelled a traitor, of being suspected of disavowing our cruel games with Vollard. It was not until evening that I finally inspected my booty and slowly decoded a passage, which turned out to be of no particular interest.

Was it that night that I dreamed that I went up to him? He was alone under a tree. Reading as usual, pouting slightly, mouth half-open, furrowing his brow. When a snapping twig called attention to my presence, he lifted his head and smiled his luminous smile as though pleased to see me. In my dream we didn't actually speak. He gestured towards a cache of wonderful books in a hollow of the tree. With a thrust of the chin he seemed to be saying: take them, they're yours to read.

[67]

The next day, deeply mortified by this dream, I was over-eager to play the cop along with the other bullies, hounding and baiting our robber-Vollard. So I acted my role of dirty little coyote rounding on a solitary sheep. Going through the motions made me feel worse than ever, for I was hopelessly drawn to Vollard's extraordinary combination of latent force, prodigious memory and the magic power to conjure up new books every day, in which he would immerse himself the moment we left him alone.

Bad feeling: not realising the extent of one's self-loathing. Bad faith: ignoring the awareness that one is colluding with an outburst of viciousness which, by threads of blood and saliva, is connected with all the cruelties in the world, even the most heinous. Children, in gangs, have a talent for that. Their presumed innocence is also a way for them to commit innocent acts of brutality.

Beyond my fascination for Vollard's reading habits there may well have been something else that intrigued me. At the lycée rumour had it that he had lived abroad before his arrival in "the metropolis". So he had known the enigmatic, dazzling light on things, the smell of dust and spices, lilting voices in alleyways and endless evenings on beaches lapped by waves, but most of all it meant that he had lived through "the war", although nobody called it that yet at the time. It was whispered at the lycée, with urgent secrecy and a kind of trepidation, that Vollard's parents, both of whom were schoolteachers, had inexplicably had their throats slashed in the night while their son lay sleeping. Atrocities such as those were daily fare where he came from, atrocities that the youngsters back home in the shelter of their old lycée could not imagine. Screams, shots, torture, massacres, throats slit and other things even more horrible. There was no end to the rumours. What had this overgrown boy experienced, what was he trying to forget, what was he after with his constant reading? What blood-curdling secrets bled behind his pages?

The day when Vollard finally put an end to his dumb martyrdom which had dragged on from one break-time to the next, when all at once he showed his mettle, I was filled with the most intense, almost physical pleasure. I almost wished it had been me he had picked on to tear to shreds.

There he was once again with his tormentors standing around him in a tight circle, jeering and shouting: "Go on, Vollard, recite!" "Watch out for your bum!" someone yelled, brandishing a pair of compasses. "I've still got a handful of hair from last time!" sneered a rat-faced little runt with grubby fingernails.

But Vollard has nothing to say. He draws himself up to his full height, flames leaping from his massive forehead. Says nothing. Fixes each boy in turn with a dark, glowering stare. No-one notices the grim tension gathering and mounting in the core of him. The jeers and taunts continue. "Well, tub of lard, had a memory loss, eh? Wanna do a runner, do you?" But there is still no response from Vollard, who merely begins to turn round very slowly while the circle widens by degrees.

Suddenly he lunges at one of the pupils, with one of his huge paws grabs him by the collar and twists the fabric of his shirt so hard that the boy is left gasping for breath, unable to speak. Next he swings his other hand to seize the one with the compasses – not that he would dream of using them now. Vollard holds out the two red-faced boys at arm's length, shaking them, plucking them up off the ground. The onlookers draw back, sniggering half-heartedly, then lapsing into silence. Vollard takes a step forward, then another, using his victims as battering rams against anyone not nimble enough to have retreated from his path. And on he goes, twisting, strangling, shaking his erstwhile tormentors who are now transformed into gurgling rag-dolls.

He marches forward. He seems strangely calm yet determined. He heads toward the concrete wall where, each break-time, we gather by the dozen to pee side by side. Vollard approaches. None of us moves a muscle. We have ceased to be members of a pack. Cops and connivers have become fearful and friendless.

Vollard stops in front of the long pissing-wall, holding up for our observation a contorted, tear-streaked face at the end of each arm. I tell myself he will kill them. That does not bother me, though there is a niggling disappointment: why didn't Vollard pick on me? Haven't I been just as foul to him as the others? Didn't I rip up one of his books?

Now Vollard turns his back on us again. Still clutching his two victims, he dashes their heads against the wall, grinds their faces into the rough concrete while the running water washes away the blood streaming from their noses. He holds them there, in the stink of stale piss, for what seems an eternity. Then, after a final shake, he lets go, and all gets mortal quiet. Each man for himself. Everyone slinks off to fight another day.

In the meantime Vollard, still with his back to us, takes a leisurely piss. A few moments later he is reading again, in a corner of the playground. No-one would take it into their head to harass him now. No-one would harass him ever again. The two battered pupils do not dare to report him. A fog of shame hovers over the playground. No-one has any desire to speak of the incident. Subject closed. I feel sick to my stomach. Would that I had choked and bled, too.

Later, we learnt that Vollard had been taken out of school, that he had gone to live in some other home, in some other town.

One detail comes back to me. Is it a detail? For many years I kept a page that was ripped from a book of Vollard's during one of our pogroms. A carefully smoothed page, read and re-read in the vain hope of unlocking its secret. It must have come from a book of Greek myths and legends, because the text introduced me to Daedalus, the skilful artificer of the very labyrinth in which he came to be imprisoned. His son Icarus, too, rose up from the page – Icarus, who had the adventure foisted on him, reluctantly obeying his father's wishes.

I read more about Daedalus' other invention, the flying machine which he fashioned for their getaway. Bird feathers, resin, branches: a contraption with huge wings that would assure freedom from any species of captivity.

My stolen page ended with Daedalus serenely taking flight, winging his way aloft, flying high enough to avoid the walls but not so high as to melt the wax securing the feathers. For a long time I associated the memory of Vollard with these mythological images. Vollard–Daedalus! The labyrinth of phrases once read and then cemented in memory . . . Vollard–Icarus! The dread of tens of thousands of memorised lines. The longing for lightness.

Vollard–Icarus soaring up into the blue sky, basking in the warm light, then tumbling, his wings ripped off, plummeting into the bitter abyss. That is how some people light upon our lives – depositing countless grubs on their way. They lay their eggs – with unforeseeable consequences – and then vanish while the grubs or the eggs look as though they are dying or decomposing. But one day . . .

Three Sightings

The next time Vollard crossed my path (had I but had such a thing!) was in Paris, during those months of May and June which, so they say, marked our youth as a generation. I recall a blizzard of black gestures and bright-red words. Days that had the joyful feeling of never ending, of running together into a single long-drawn-out day filled with radical endeavours. I recall nights of violence spilling into the daytime, and days, ever new, sliding sardonically into night. I recall unprecedented ways of relating to other bodies, to space, to time.

When I think back on those times it is not Vollard who comes to mind. He tends to be forgotten, blotted out. And yet . . .

What I remember most vividly are the crowds. The feeling that we were permanently at the hub of huge knots of people. People, masses of people, a sense of knowing everybody, of at once finding the centre of each gathering. The shadow of the seething mob, throbbing almost like a heart, advancing in a fog of words, slogans, fists, gaping mouths, bodies offering themselves like fruit, open shirts, grimy hands, perpendicular streets, thousands of red helmets thrust up in the sunlight. The crowd and the tumult repeatedly torn apart by tear gas and ambulance sirens.

Something in me wants to forget that Vollard was there, he too. I recognised him immediately by his size, his girth, his red hair, his hands, his fists. Something in me wants to forget having spotted him and observed him at length, as I did on three occasions and in the most emblematic settings of that historic spring episode, on this stage of nighttime riotings. Why forget his presence if he was simply there, like a reminder, a landmark, a great rusty bollard, an extinguished beacon sporadically spreading a light of sorts?

I must admit that I still do my best to conjure the sense of immediacy and openness of those days. I cherish the memory of a breach through which a great gust of fresh air blew upon us, an air previously unknown, musical and bright, a luminous filament, a tightrope that we were able to walk without having learnt. But the mood was also one of the grossest over-simplifications, of sweeping magical-historical statements, and we confused, in all innocence, the two faces of the easy way out: luck and great idleness.

I kept pace with the ebb and flow of those days; proper reading didn't come into it. Not once during that spring did I take the time to read a book, although I was a habitual, dedicated reader. Where and when would I have done so? There was the urgency of adventure. Always something on the go. Always something new.

Time expanded while a kind of mass intoxication took over – joint actions, meetings, public debates, organisations and collectives – which left no room for solitude and singularity. Should that have put us on our guard? Even the anarchy was a group activity.

So what of Vollard? Catching sight of him in the midst of a dense, motley crowd filling the large quadrangle of the student-occupied Sorbonne gave me a shock. For it was undeniably him. There was not the slightest doubt in my mind, even though I had not seen him since his sudden departure from our lycée, when at fourteen he was already man-sized, with those huge boots of his, those great hands and arms, the bushy red hair and the thick glasses. There he was, at the Sorbonne, seven years later!

What was he up to in those hectic days? What was Vollard up to when the activism was at its height, when all those crowds were gathering and dispersing and gathering again, when the walls were being daubed with slogans, like arrows, on the button, in black brushstrokes, and everywhere tracts and leaflets? What was he up to when those long-winded circulars stuck up on the present to herald the future were being dashed off and roneoed at top speed? What was Vollard doing when young, self-styled nurses tended to the wounded, and girls with flowing manes heckled overgrown boys who were letting their hair grow, when everyone was talking at the same time, debating what anyone was proposing, denouncing, proclaiming?

I was in that crowd at the Sorbonne, mildly drunk on the sense of a vast, inchoate "us" bristling with ideas, gestures and voices. No doubt an illusory "us", but one that had been unimaginable until a very short time before.

[75]

That was when I spotted Vollard. Why was it so unsettling? In those turbulent times you were forever running into people you had met at one time or another. Faces you had lost sight of years ago, matured but younger-looking, suddenly stood out from the thousand-strong others.

He was standing on the steps leading to the chapel, one shoulder propped against the handbill-covered pedestal of Victor Hugo's statue. A lone, towering figure in a big shapeless jacket, one leg crossed over the other, head bowed, pensive and apparently indifferent to everything happening around him. Étienne Vollard was reading. He was reading with the same tranquillity as if he'd been out on a moor somewhere or a river bank, engrossed in a book which, in his spade-like hands, looked tiny but precious.

Stationed thus at the top of the steps, Vollard dominated the swirling multitude and cacophony of words. He was a living sculpture leaning with his back against the statue of a writer become invisible. Vollard was reading the way I had seen him read in the school playground. He was reading as if he were standing by a large open window. Up in the mountains. By the sea.

He inhabited a remote inner space, while we on the outside were causing a somewhat ludicrous ruckus. I approached him, in the lee of all the bodies occupied with occupying the Sorbonne.

From the start of the affair I had, naively, been persuaded of the harmony of what we were doing, that we were living day by day with something we called History, and the shock of seeing Vollard that day caused a strange rift in my awareness, a crack that zigzagged away and branched out to join another, previous fissure before widening imperceptibly.

I was wrapped up in the bliss that was this historical moment. But the sight of Vollard unnerved me, robbing me of all sense of commitment and belonging. What was going on? Images gushed forth like bad blood: Vollard being compelled to recite under a hail of jibes, Vollard being hounded to exhaustion, the compass points, the kicks, the peals of laughter. His books snatched from him, ripped. Him being heaved out of the window. But it all went deeper than that. Under the surface of shame there was the dream I once had of Vollard showing me the cache of books in the hollow tree, and the longing to read like him, to find out what he was reading, to claim it for myself, discover its secret. Deeper down still was my juvenile satisfaction at seeing him make his tormentors bleed from the head, at Vollard being capable of throttling, of killing quite calmly but also, just as calmly, of restraining himself.

At one point I found myself in front of the statue of Victor Hugo, right beneath Vollard who, to be sure, was still reading. If he had looked up from his book, would he have recognised me? I wonder. Not for a moment did it occur to me to accost him. Talk to him? In the name of such painful memories? No! I had nothing to say. There was nothing between us. We were on different planets. My only reason for drawing near was to see what was the book Vollard was able to be reading there, on his own, in the May sunshine. For it dawned on me then, with unaccountable certainty, that the sense, if there was a sense to be found at all, that the sense of things, of our lives, of what was going on, was not enshrined in the actions and words of a young rebellious crowd; no indeed, the sense, such as it was – obscure, discreet, troubling – was right there, staring me in the face: black on white, in the pages Vollard shielded with his body like a gem. Mysterious, radioactive pages.

That was as far as I got, because just then Vollard shook himself like a great lumbering beast, bear-dog or sphinx-platypus, and he glanced around with a kindly, rather forlorn air while a very pretty girl brushed past him going down the steps. Then he smiled the same luminous smile I had seen in my boyhood dream. I realised that, in his own way, he was alert to his surroundings, for just as there is the vantage point of the "prone gunman", his was that of the "reader standing".

He slipped the book into the pocket of his jacket and shambled off through the crowd towards the boisterous streets of the Latin Quarter. I did not attempt to follow him. The question of what he had been reading with such close attention remained unanswered.

I had other sightings of Vollard during this feverish spring. Sightings? Visions? One time I suddenly thought I recognised him standing right near me in the carnavalesque crowd that had just occupied the Odéon theatre. Vollard was both aloof and in the thick of things, reading as usual, head bent forward, but strangely attentive all the same. The nuances and colours of everything happening around him were all swept up into the great white hole of the books he carried everywhere with him.

Vision? Hallucination? No, it was him all right, the guy with the red hair and beard, a head taller than everyone else at the permanently provisional assembly. When he raised his eyes behind their bottle glasses he seemed to be examining the faces and gesticulations with an extraordinary intensity and a kind of wonder.

Out of the blue, in the hubbub, in the methodical chaos of the gathering, Vollard was singled out by an excited young self-appointed chairman who was trying hard to keep the meeting from disintegrating.

"The comrade over there has something to say!" he shouted, pointing to Vollard, who had indicated no such thing but may have made a vague gesture.

Why this short-term chairman should have chosen to give the floor to Vollard when there were dozens of arms being waved for attention was unclear.

"Yes, our friend with the red hair, over there . . . Go on, comrade, speak! We're listening."

I remember Vollard's reaction as one of acute bewilderment as he raised his head and lowered his book. Hundreds of attentive faces turned to him in a semblance of silence.

Vollard muttered something like: "I'm not your comrade . . . And I don't have anything to say."

But the impromptu leader insisted, and Vollard drew himself up to his full height, looming over the crowd. He smiled and came out with the following bizarre, incongruous statement: "I didn't ask anything. Least of all to speak. I prefer silence. You carry on with your discussions . . . I have nothing to say."

The crowd heard what Vollard said, but they did not listen. A strange mist of tolerance hung over these tumultuous gatherings. Speaking out was paramount, but what was said went unheeded in the maelstrom. More hue and cry. More statements, more proclamations. On completely different topics.

Meanwhile, in the immediate vicinity of Vollard, a mixture of indignation and qualified approval. Someone said, "If you've nothing to say, comrade, just shut up!" "No, comrade," another said. "It's OK to say you have nothing to say."

And Vollard laughed as if it were a good joke before immersing himself in his book once more. "*It is my dearest art and my dearest mischief to have taught my silence not to betray itself by silence.*"

Must I summon up my third sighting of Vollard during that remarkable spring? A memory that is both moving and disturbing? It was one of the last nights of rioting, a night like so many others, except that this one was excessive and bitter. The violence had spread all over the city. Left Bank. Right Bank. Makeshift barricades. Bonfires. Troops deployed, a colourful throng, but determined. Catcalls, shouts, then the serried ranks of black helmets, hostile, bristling with guns and truncheons. The gleam of metal. Explosions. Smoke. And before long, ambulance sirens.

On the right bank the mob, in considerable confusion, is beating a slow retreat down an avenue. Missiles flying through the air. Deafening explosions of grenades. The first bodies falling to the ground. The first bloodshed. Youngsters protecting their heads with both hands, sticky with red. During a brutal charge, four or five riot police bear down on a boy lying sprawled on the asphalt, just ahead of the crowd which is receding in a suffocating fog. They beat the boy with truncheons, drag him by his hair, by his collar, towards the big Black Marias that are rolling into view. Suddenly, through my stinging tears, I see Vollard. Huge. Hair on end. Wearing his perennial jacket. Was it him? In that stampede? A case of Reader Encounters Riot? An actor? Ghost at the feast? Even today the mystery survives. I see him break away from the front line and stride towards the policemen. He catches up with them, shoves them aside, grabs the unconscious boy, scoops him up with one arm, and wards off the truncheon blows raining down on him by flailing his left fist, thrusting his shoulders, kicking out with his boots, as a result of which two policemen fall to the ground. Slowly, he makes his way back to the crowd, which the isolated policemen will not charge again. Hands reach out to take the injured boy, run him to the ambulances. Vollard vanishes. Engulfed by an emblematic cloud of smoke.

The Company of Writers

Imagine my surprise, having reluctantly taken up a post in that city hemmed in by mountains, at coming upon Vollard. I recognised him at once. He was quite a bit older, of course, stouter too and stiffer in the joints, but still the same: head bent forward, brow resting on his fist, ensconced among his books – all of them, the books on their wooden shelves and the books in his head. Vollard had become a bookseller. He had found himself a niche: "The Verb To Be". Had he fetched up in this corner of France by chance, like me, or was it his choice?

So it happened that, a few months before he ran over the little girl, I saw Étienne Vollard again. The town was quite new to me, and I went for long walks every day to explore. I didn't yet dare raise my eyes to the mountains, let alone hike up the paths to the summits you could see from every street corner. First I needed some assurance that I would not be too lonely there, that I would be able to breathe, and it was in libraries and bookshops that I went looking for oxygen. Public libraries, bookshops large and small, I visited each one in turn to discover where I might feel most at home in the months to come, the years maybe.

It was not long before I was drawn to a modest bookshop with a sign saying THE VERB TO BE – BOOKS, NEW AND

SECOND-HAND. The glazed door had a handle shaped like the ridged spine of a leather-bound book, which gave a pleasing sensation when gripped. "Push!" it said. Inside, there was coolness and depth, shadows and pools of light.

Poring over the books on display, examining the titles on the shelves, I did not at first notice Vollard. A small, sere woman dressed in black, a cigarette between her lips, inquired discreetly whether I needed any help. I was happy to browse, and was about to start when I heard a loud clearing of the throat followed by a cavernous cough.

Vollard was seated behind a plain wooden table surrounded by yet more towers of books. A huge surprise. The return of a deeply buried past. Swelling up before me was the living embodiment of my first, conscience-stricken encounter with the power of reading. It was him. Here! Thirty-seven years later.

He stirred convulsively and heaved himself to his feet, bullish and hefty, more burdened than ever with the texts banked in his memory. He paid no attention to me. With a grim expression he seized a weighty volume which he hefted in his hands and then began to read, eyes glinting behind his glasses. Still reading, he sank down again behind the table into an armchair which sagged under his weight. My eyes became adjusted to the complicated pattern of dimness and light, and it was then I saw that Vollard – head down, breathing heavily – was surrounded by pictures of authors tacked up on the wall. Portraits in black and white of famous writers in memorable poses.

To the right of the bookseller's shoulder I recognised the strained look of Dostoevsky. A photograph taken just before the end: vast forehead taking up half the dome of the skull, the sunken, wild eyes already fixed on death, long eyebrows, and the beard, still very dark with a few crinkly strands of white.

Close by, a grainy picture of Malcolm Lowry in profile, alone, on the bank of a dark lake, with that disconsolate air of his, the lost look, the pale trousers, the polo shirt stretched over the paunch swollen with tequila and mescal, a mass of words and emotion on a rock, surrounded by silence. "*No, you do not understand me if you think all I see is darkness.*"

And Céline: shabby coat thrown over the shoulders as if he is cold, crumpled silk scarf around his neck, ill shaven, black and white stubble beneath the nose, on the cheeks, and beneath the mouth which has lost none of its firmness, but the eyes are averted and the brow furrowed, in a sort of weary surprise, vexed and weary.

On the wall immediately behind Vollard was the portrait of Henry Miller as lecherous old fossil, skull shiny with age, eyes narrowed like a cat's, the stirring of a smile on his full lips, lined face burnished by a lifetime of dedication to work and debauchery, a contented vitality, both sexual and literary.

Then there was the shot of Georges Bataille seemingly taken unawares: meat-eater's mouth, pale angelic eyes that speak of purity and also sickness, a shock of white hair with a rebellious tuft like an alien's antenna, and that air of his of

[84]

being elsewhere, of angelic sadness – part suffering, part infancy – contrasting with the absurd elegance of his suit and black tie: "*I write for anyone who, having stumbled on my book, falls into a hole he will never climb out of.*"

And Max Frisch, thickset and abundant, in shirt sleeves at an empty pavement café, outsize black-framed spectacles like portholes, a pipe dangling from his mouth, hands waving, explaining something to someone outside the picture: "*One can tell any story but one's own.*"

Hemingway: elderly, grizzled colossus, jutting paunch. All the demons and the wounds and the sorrows hidden away under the pathetic veneer of a Hollywood actor's mug offering itself to the bottle, and finally to the barrel of the gun that will blow it away.

There were so many faces surrounding the bookseller: Artaud, Kafka, Borges, Pessoa, Beckett, Nabokov, Thomas Mann, Pavese, and I could not help conflating their features with those of Vollard, until he turned into a robot portrait of all the writers whose works slumbered in his memory.

I spoke very little with Vollard, who was understandably disinclined to recognise in me one of his hateful "mates" from the old days (maybe he did, though), but once I had become a regular customer at the "The Verb To Be", the long thin city hemmed in by mountains became strangely more appealing.

Every two or three days I would go up to him, seated behind his table, with a few books, either new or used, and these I would hand to him along with some banknotes. He

[85]

would take his time, nod or shake his head, or he would smile with a kind of childish glee at my choice, after which he would stuff my money into the cigar box in front of him and give me my change with a grunt. More than once he concluded the transaction by launching into a quote of some length which, needless to say, came from the very book I had just paid for. He recited from memory, but only to himself, under his breath. An unnerving experience the first time, but somewhat to my surprise I soon found myself looking forward to these impromptu performances.

I got to know Madame Pélagie, with whom conversation was easier than with Vollard, and some of the clientele, including the famed Boncassa running the gamut of books until closing time. An inveterate reader, Boncassa claimed that the time he didn't spend reading was taken up editing a magnificent opus that would make its mark on the world, a work he had been engaged in for more than thirty years, and beside which *In Search of Lost Time, The Human Comedy,* and *The Divine Comedy* would pale into insignificance!

So I settled into a sort of habit: my long tramps across the city invariably wound up at "The Verb To Be", and in the end Vollard took on the stature of a monument of flesh and memory, a pulsing, secret textual cathedral, ironically and fortuitously erected on this square in the old town. A spiritual hitching-post, an intellectual necessity, in a town with so little else to recommend it.

How could I have foreseen what would happen?

PART III

Insomnia

After the accident, after the night spent screaming on the mountain and smacking his head against low-hanging branches, after the endless day in the district hospital waiting for the comatose body of a child in the company of a young woman desperate to "run away", Vollard had returned home on foot, in the snow and fog, to the old town. Incapable of showing his face in "The Verb To Be", he had sought refuge in his flat.

He had not made an appearance for two days, but Madame Pélagie was accustomed to Vollard's absences, his sudden departures, his eventful returns. He often travelled to other towns – sometimes quite a distance away – to attend antiquarian book sales. Or he would shut himself up at home for as long as it took to read a particularly long novel. No-one kept track of his comings and goings. He would also go hiking in the mountains of the Grande Chartreuse to get rid of his dangerous energy. After walking for hours, burning off the violence of the past, he would settle down among the rocky crags for some more reading, in wind, rain and snow at times, huddled under his black umbrella. Saint Jerome in a red cape, a giant ape poring over the Scriptures. *"Haw! How it all comes back to me, to be sure. That look! That weary watchful vacancy! The man arrives! The dark ways all behind, all within, the long dark ways, in his head, in his side, in his hands and feet, and he sits in the rosy gloom, picking his nose, waiting for the dawn to break. The dawn! The sun! The light! Haw! The long blue days for his head, for his side, and the little paths for his feet, and all the brightness to touch and gather."*

Arriving home he was overcome by thirst. First he drank water, litres of water which he took from the bottle, letting it pour down his neck and on to his chest. His torn and smelly clothes lay strewn at his feet.

Stark naked, ashen-faced and freckled, covered in bruises and scratches, he poured himself a glass of whisky, a second, and then a third, which he took with him to the shower. He crouched under the scalding jets in the steam and made himself small, a thick slab of sad meat with water drumming on the outside and alcohol coursing inside. How long he stayed like that he did not know. Soaked and dripping water everywhere, he finally threw himself on to his bed and fell into an inordinately deep, mindless sleep, the sleep of a child. So deeply asleep, unreachable by nightmares, visions, and especially by the sentences which, most nights, surged into his mind to keep him awake. Because insomnia – blinding, tormenting insomnia – was something Vollard suffered from long before the accident. Night after night, year after year. Insomnia encourages reading. Which exacerbates insomnia.

What happened that evening, after the accident, the snow, the night spent on the mountain and the day at the hospital? The long-standing insomniac Vollard fell face down in a cess-pit of thick black slurry that clogged up the holes in his skull and prevented them squirting all those phosphorescent sentences from the archives of his sleepless brain.

For many years, night after night, however late it might be, it was always thus: no sooner had Vollard put his book down, snapped off the light and shut his eyes than the insomnia switched another light on in his head, brighter and more glaring. The insomnia forced on him other sentences, born of anguish and of memory.

During these long spells of wakefulness there was, at first, the "weird voice" making itself heard in the dark, half growling and half squealing entreaties like: "Not me! Not that!" It was not quite his own voice, but oddly familiar none the less, could be that of a boy whose voice is breaking so that the sounds come out too high or too low.

"Please don't! Not me! Not that!" the voice would exclaim. Or plead: "Stop! That's enough now!" It was the voice of a child, moaning in the sleepless night. Its cry of "Not me, not that!" sounded exactly like the throttled tones of "Maman", the word silently mouthed by young and old alike, stifled in the dark, a hoarse "Maman" for lack of tears, while at the other end of the boundless night an absent mother, lost mother, dead mother, laments that she is only a child herself, that there is no mother, anywhere, no grown-ups at all, none but the eternal child, the eternal little girl . . .

Then, in an effort to screen out the "weird voice", more sentences would crawl out of the holes. There were thousands of texts packed in the great skein of Vollard's

[91]

remembrance. Thousands of phrases unravelling, lighting up the dark, smothering the unceasing entreaties of "Enough! Not me! Not that!" Lines plucked from every book read since childhood, a relentless tide of sentences permanently housed in Vollard's skull.

The anguished voice persisted in its supplication while the phrases streamed fast and furious: *"Iron, it must be made of iron, this night, supported by huge flying buttresses so as to resist the onslaught of all those things my wounded eyes have seen, of the things that so horribly people the night."*

"Enough is enough!" repeated the anguished voice. And the other spoke:

> *"Come, most ancient and identical Night,*
> *Night Queen by birth dethroned*
> *Night whose core is silence, Night*
> *Like the stars slow and fast*
> *On your dress fringed with Infinity.*
> *Come vaguely,*
> *Come lightly*
> *Come alone . . .".*

Howls from the anguished voice. A duel in the night. More sentences. On and on until the rotten dawn. Reader Jekyll versus Mister Nightmare.

> *"Carry me off in a caravel,*
> *In an ancient and sweet caravel,*

In the prow or if you like in the foam,
And lose me far, far away . . . "

But there was no caravel in sight. This insomnia had no horizon. The anguished voice went on: "Enough! That's enough! Take me away, Maman caravel . . . You know I need you a thousand times more now that I am getting old, a thousand times more do I need your hull and your arms, Maman, even if you are dead, even if you have shrunk to a little girl yourself, crying out, like me, at the other end of this night so unlike night."

The other voice riposted: "*I have more memories in myself alone than all men have had since the world was a world. My dreams are like your waking hours. My memory, señor, is like a garbage heap.*"

Towards daybreak Vollard would finally drift into a troubled sleep, only to be woken an hour or two later by a nightmare or a ray of light, whereupon he would sit bolt upright, upsetting the piles of books about his rumpled bed. Books on the bedside table, books on all the furniture. Books trailing into the bathroom, the kitchen, gathering dust in the shadows.

Confronting his own reflection always gave Vollard the same surprise. Sunken, dark-rimmed eyes, no glasses, in the middle of a big blotch, pale and whiskery. Ageless. Naked in the stillness. Solitude of flesh: sex, stomach, thighs. Bits and pieces of thoughts.

And then, at the approach of dawn, the sentences would

one by one fall silent. A precarious truce. *"My memory, señor, is like a garbage heap..."*

Morning at last! Time for Vollard to consume fresh supplies of print over a good half litre of coffee. There would be books waiting all around him. Stacks of them. New and old.

The fact remains that this first sleep after the accident was exceptional. Proper, deep sleep! Vollard lingered on in his liquid torpor, wading through the last shallows of blackness until, suddenly, he was on his feet, with the memory of the accident boring itself into his skull while the orchestra of the catastrophe struck up in full force.

Mouth parched, hands outstretched, he picked his way across the room, hampered by the books, empty bottles, medicine wrappers strewn about the floor. He had the strange sensation that from now on it would be his own hands that would hamper him. Never again would they reach out and touch in the same way. The hands of a killer. *Hands of Orlac.*

And so, from one moment to the next, it is possible to find oneself ranked among murderers. A primordial violence had returned, a deep-seated violence, and with it the old "killer instinct".

The morning was half gone when he came down to the shop, where Madame Pélagie often was since eight a.m. even though she did not open until nine sharp. She saw to the invoices, sorted books and took receipt of deliveries.

[94]

She was always there, alert and attentive. In her own way she, too, was a memory bank. But hers was an efficient memory, not a garbage heap. You could ask her the reference of a book that was out of print, the name of an author if you could supply a fraction of the title, or the exact title of a book if you gave her a garbled version. After some swift searches, she always managed to come up with the correct answer: "No, monsieur, not *La Méduse* by Georges Goubet, what you mean is *L'Hydre* by Guillaume Loubet . . ."

Every evening, after closing time, she would slip two or three books in cellophane wrappers to take home. She was an omnivorous reader, and very fast, by a diagonal method of her own devising. She read at random, never communicating her preferences, such as they were, to anyone. She was driven by a sense of professional duty, by the will to come up with her own résumé or personal comment for any given book, whether a study of animal language, a philosophical essay or a many-faceted novel. There was not a title in stock that she had nothing to say about, nor was she above the most bewildering improvisations, complex narrations, or acrobatic simplifications in her resolve to give the customer a notion of the contents.

That morning, Vollard came in by the back door. The shop was empty but for Madame Pélagie, whom he greeted with a grunt. He seemed not to notice the newly unpacked books: new publications, new editions, topical biographies, first novels. Normally the sight of brand-new books in their open cartons would bring a curiously sensual glow to his face, and his lips would almost curl with eagerness. Also he liked gutting the boxes with a single slice of the cutter and gathering up the books in his arms as if they were pulsing with life, pissing their sentences like blood. Always the same eagerness. Even after so many years. Tingling with anticipation, Vollard would take the paper blocks in his hands, run his fingers over them, scrutinise them, turn them over, open them feverishly, inhale the smell of glue and paper, and before long he would be turning the pages with bated breath and razor eyes, drawing rapid but pertinent conclusions, whereafter he would select several titles for his night-time reading.

Madame Pélagie saw at once that something was seriously wrong, but she went about her businesses without comment. She had to fight the urge to ask, "What's the matter with you today? What is it, Étienne? What's wrong?" She knew in her bones that it was neither insomnia, nor one of his migraines or indigestion, nor a book he could not stomach or a particularly riveting read which was troubling the bookseller. There was something very disturbing about the way Vollard lumbered down the aisles without pausing to touch a single book.

He wrenched open the front door and vanished into the street, where the air was filled with the clang of snow shovels clearing the pavements.

The Plaster Mask

On the hospital road the snow was churned to a foul slush by
tyres and footsteps. Beige slurry liquefying by the hour. There
was no end to the stream of visitors approaching this fortress
stockpiled with mutilated bodies and diseased organisms,
with lives on the brink, kept going for just a little longer by
machines. Bodies with perforations, injections, plaster casts.
Newborn babies too, the premature ones, impatient for life.
Vollard glanced up at the narrow rectangles with lowered
blinds, trying to make out which window concealed the little
girl. Was she still breathing? Had she opened her eyes? He
picked his way hurriedly through the slush, taking care not to
bump into anyone in the snow-dazed crowd in case they
slipped and fell.

The glass doors gave a soft mewing sound as they parted
automatically at his approach, even as he needlessly held out
his arms. He stepped into the opaque aquarium of the large
hall, already very busy at this hour. Green plants trailed like
algae under milky strip lights. All manner of people floated
in these unquiet waters, shoaling at different speeds: stubbly
men in pyjamas, women with shaved heads in dressing
gowns, dead cigarettes between their lips, hasty young
women in white, warmly wrapped old people, visitors
uncertain where to go . . .

Suddenly, in the milling crowd, Vollard spotted Thérèse Blanchot, the little girl's mother. She would have gone straight past him, hurrying towards the exit with her hand on her chest as if she were suffocating and in need of fresh air. He caught her by the elbow.

"Are you leaving your daughter? How is she?"

He held her back, pulling her towards him. Her small hands struggled to push away Vollard's great red paw, but he would not let go, implacable.

"No change . . . Her breathing's regular, but she hasn't moved. She's just lying there, like when you saw her. So pale. Her arms . . . I'd never noticed how thin they are."

"Are you leaving?"

"What do you want me to do?"

"But they said—"

"That I should talk to her? Yes, they say it's important to keep talking to her, all the time. But I just can't do it. I really tried . . ."

"So?"

"As soon as I start telling her something, doesn't matter what, it's as if I'm scared that she'll hear. You know, that she can hear me but that she won't say anything back."

Having wriggled free from Vollard's hold, Thérèse took a small step, then another, in the direction of the exit.

"I'm sorry," she said hurriedly, "but I did stay with Éva for a long time. It's just that I need a breather right now. A

[98]

smoke. I thought I'd get my car, drive around for a bit. But I'll be back, you know, I'll be back . . . Listen, why don't you have a go talking to her?"

With that Thérèse fled, leaving Vollard absurdly stranded in the middle of the crowd. Deciding against taking one of the six slow, crowded lifts, he started up the stairs, heaving his one hundred and ten kilos up to the floor of mangled bodies, broken limbs, smashed skulls, puffed-up flesh. He needed to release some physical and mental energy before seeing the child again.

Going down the passage to Éva's room, he knocked his thigh against a steel trolley, rattling its load of bottles, instruments, boxes of dressings. The noise made a nurse swing round, ready to remonstrate, but she recognised the big man and her face softened to a smile of sincere or professional compassion:

"Ah, here's our little girl's daddy, our little Éva. That's good. You can talk to her. Just go on talking, keep it up. Stimulate her. Tell yourself she can hear you, that she'll hear you eventually, that she's there."

"But I'm not her . . . " faltered Vollard.

"Sit yourself up close to your daughter's ear, and you'll see . . . "

Imagine! Him, her father! Impostor, more like. Dangerous driver posing as devoted father. His wretchedness increased tenfold. The horror of this bogus father's hands and body drawing near to the comatose daughter of a stranger! At the same time his distress at this borrowed paternity, this paternity foisted on him by chance, did hold out a mysterious fascination.

He leaned over very slightly towards the waxen face of the child. The body lay under a white sheet with the bare arms exposed. Little, stick-like arms, pale and breakable, extremely fine fingers lying utterly still, hardly any fingernails.

The eyes were shut, as before, the forehead wide and smooth. The oxygen mask had been removed. What struck Vollard this time was how like a princess she looked, the impressive calm, thanks no doubt to the head clamp and the bandage like a turban. The child had lapsed into an extended swoon, a magical slumber of seven years, or of a hundred. Under a spell.

He did not touch her, did not even brush against her, but almost in spite of himself he leaned closer to the little black holes of her flared nostrils, hoping to detect a breath or tremor.

For a long time he sat there on the metal chair, watching over this unconsciousness, this vacancy that was more compelling than any mobile, sentient body could ever have been. For all the absence of movement, it was still the same child whose terrified eyes had held his own through the windscreen. Where was that look of terror now? Had it been shattered, like glass?

With his lips close to the child's smooth cheek, Vollard was startled by the sound of his own breathing disturbing the silence in the room. He drew back.

He had wanted to speak, but the wrong words kept

coming up, assembling into phrases he could not utter. He could not say: "It's me, I'm the one who did this to you. It was me, you know, that cold rainy evening when you sprang into the road. Saw you too late . . . Couldn't do a thing . . . But why were you running like that, for heaven's sake? You were crying . . . Our eyes met, don't you remember? There was no stopping. No way at all."

So he said nothing.

Anyone who has ever pleaded "Don't die!" with someone they love, someone who is no longer listening, who is slipping away, keeling over to the other side, too far away already to reply, anyone who has ever screamed without a sound passing their lips, "Don't die, don't leave me, not just yet," or who has begged, "Please, please open your eyes just one more time, tell me you can hear me, give me a sign, move a finger, just a fraction . . . don't die!" will have some idea of what was going through Vollard's mind.

But he said none of these things. There was only the sound of his own breathing, the boorish rasp in his throat. A burden unto himself. Heavier and more crushing than ever.

Time passed. Nurses slipped into the room, performed small tasks, checked the monitors, slipped out again. Vollard stayed. And Thérèse did not come back.

Silence. Face of a princess. Plaster mask. Suddenly a stream of words resonated in the room. Sure enough, it was Vollard uttering them. A loud, strong voice, articulating clearly a text retained from long ago. In his mind's eye Vollard could distinctly see the old edition, printed in grey

Garamond on poor-quality paper. Also the brown stains in the margins.

"*You would have taken her for an angel, so beautiful was she; . . . her eyes were closed, but you could hear her gentle breathing, which proved that she was not dead. The King decreed that she should be left to sleep in peace until such time as her waking hour had struck. Then the good fairy, who had saved her life by sending her to sleep for a hundred years . . .*"

To his surprise, Vollard found himself telling a story to the child behind the plaster mask. He told her the first story that came to his mind. Far, far away, at the bottom of the transparent sea, there lived a princess, soft-skinned and pale in the watery blueness. She was the most beautiful of princesses, but instead of legs and feet she had a fish's tail.

Vollard felt uneasy at the sound of his own voice invading the silent room. He was a little short of breath, but carried on as if he had the printed page before him:

"*. . . often, at night, she looked up at the faint glow of the moon and the stars, and whenever they disappeared behind a dark cloud, she knew there was a whale or a ship with people on board passing overhead.*"

The words of the fairytale were like furrows in the wake of the bookseller-whale swimming high above the submerged face of a child who was neither dead nor asleep, but plunged in a coma that might endure for ever.

Ordinarily, the face of someone who listens is a little like a sponge. Infinitesimal twitches, minute contractions of the skin signal that the speaker is being heard. Even the most impenetrable stranger, even someone who is asleep, cannot stop their faces absorbing some of the words addressed to them. But Éva's face was the mask of a princess neither alive nor dead: pinched nostrils, slightly parted lips, and the cavity of the ear a minuscule labyrinth with Vollard crouching at the entrance like a puzzled Minotaur, nothing to guide him but the breakable thread of words, all unwitting of any Ariadne whom he might never reach.

The slight, still frame embodied a terrible desolation which Vollard recognised as the polar opposite of his own. It was not just the desolation of a little girl who was badly hurt and in a deep coma, it was the desolation of effacement, diminution, depletion, even her colour seeping away. The more terrible for the discretion, for the gradual obliteration.

Compared to this most undiluted of solitudes, that of a bruised, middle-aged man such as Vollard counted for little. His was due to a surfeit of flesh and of memory, to the preposterous body he had been lumbered with. He was lonely by dint of feeling in the way. A loner, too, whose solitude was laughable, or simply sad. Sorrow and suffering entwined since childhood, long ago.

No connection, then, with the sense that reality might suddenly be slurped up by this white face, by these nostrils, these parted lips. A sense that the world could swallow itself up through the body of a little girl only to be spat out again in a remote interior called Nowhere.

It was to erase this disquieting notion from his mind that, after the first tale, Vollard embarked on others, which occurred to him purely by chance but of which he had total recall. Texts evoking childhood.

"I was at that time like a fledgling swallow living high up in a niche in the eaves, who from time to time peeps out over the top of its nest with its little bright eyes and imagines, just by looking out over the yard and the road, that it is seeing the depths of the world and of space . . ."

Nurses slipped in and out on tiptoe, not wishing to interrupt Vollard, whose voice could be heard out in the corridor.

". . . then shutting the still cloudy eye of my mind, I lapsed for whole days into my tranquil, elemental night."

Vollard recited until nightfall, but came back the following afternoon, after he had spoken to Madame Pélagie at last. She had listened carefully with furrowed brow, drawing nervously on her cigarette without offering the least comment, either sympathetic or shocked, about the accident. She had simply said: "Yes, that is what you should do, Étienne. Spend time with the child. Talk to her. Take all the time you need. I'll hold the fort here."

From then on Vollard went to the hospital every day to tell his stories in a loud, clear voice. Sometimes he would bump into Thérèse – hurried, downcast, off again in no time. He kept it up for two weeks, not missing a day.

"We seem to see a lot more of you than of your lady wife," the nurse who came in the mornings remarked. "I could tell she doesn't find it easy to talk to the little girl. Shame. Because that's what she needs. You'll see, one day there'll be a change. One never knows which word or expression might rouse them. Just one sentence could do the trick. Like getting hold of one end of a thread and using it to reel all the rest back in. Coma is a very mysterious thing . . ."

On one occasion Vollard turned round to find Thérèse quietly perching on the end of her daughter's bed. He had not heard her come in. Her hair was damp, falling over her eyes, and, in spite of the heat in the room, she kept her coat on as though poised to leave. Hunched, arms crossed, all ears. Vollard studied her face as he went on talking. The resemblance with Éva suddenly struck him. So young looking. Too young. A child herself. A revenant Éva. A girl-mother.

"I was listening to you, Monsieur Vollard," Thérèse said.

"Have you been here long?"

"I really like your stories. I keep thinking I recognise things."

"Oh, they're just books I read ages ago and still remember, stuff that comes back to me . . . just like that. That's all."

"I haven't read many books, myself. And when I do read stuff, I forget it right away. I don't know why. But you're different, you . . ."

"It's no great advantage, you know, it's not even a gift. It's just memory, and I have to live with it."

"Well, I think I'll give her a kiss on her forehead and then I'll be off. I've got things to . . ."

"I know."

★

The days passed. Vollard's voice in Éva's ear grew and grew, pouring forth the words unleashed by his memory. The hospital staff left him alone.

In the streets the snow had melted, but the mountains surrounding the valley were blindingly white. Towards evening, on the darkened avenues, there was an underwater atmosphere, a sense of wading with difficulty along the bottom of a hostile ocean, while up there, not far away, the blue shimmer of the peaks invited one to climb up for a breath of air at the inaccessible surface.

The Miracle of Awakening

The loathsome Christmas season was nigh. Fairy lights, gilt, tinkling bells, stomach-turning music and the wide, compelling leer of merchandise. Indiscriminate buying, in a pretence of giving gifts. Compulsory gifts. So why not books?

Season of trade, winter exasperation. Choked streets, pavements overflowing with bundled-up pedestrians, themselves overflowing with parcels, the invariable surge of a somnambulist buying spree.

Vollard could not, as usual, help jostling people as he picked his way through the crowd, which thinned to a straggle near the hospital.

In the end it was a relief to get out of the shop, not to have to put up with the complainings of customers who do not venture into a bookshop more than once or twice a year, in search not of a book but of something to give away: "You will gift-wrap it, won't you?"

The test he set himself was different: daily walk, white hallways smelling of sickness and medicines, improvised recitation, marathon story-run. In his mind this challenge suddenly became very circumscribed and necessary, as though it were possible to cram the whole of existence into this daily shuttle between an old-fashioned bookshop and an ultra-modern hospital. Vollard had never thought of literature as soothing, nor of reading as a consolation. On the contrary. Reading with abandon, which had always been his way, had more to do with discovering the pain of someone else. The pain of a lonely man, the bewilderment of a lonely woman. Reading meant descending to the depths of their suffering and exploring it at close quarters. It meant that behind the sentences, even the most beautifully crafted ones, you could always hear the cry of anguish. Going back and forth between the bookshop and the hospital meant commuting between two kinds of trauma. The murmur and woe of the books ranged on their shelves at one end, and at the other the moans of those who had passed in a split second from able-bodied insouciance to amputation, from hale and hearty to the ravages of terminal disease. Walking quickly, head down, hands thrust deep in his pockets or swinging in the air like paddles, Vollard felt himself maintaining a strange liaison between two distinct universes. All the rest – the pedestrian bustle, the shopping, Christmas, food, traffic jams – went round and round in circles of unreality.

When Vollard was a long time getting back from the hospital, Madame Pélagie would keep the shop open after the closing hour. She welcomed latecomers, and if there were none she would listen patiently to Boncassa, who never gave up disparaging world literature, "killing off" new authors as well as nearly all the old ones, railing against publishers and especially the buying public, who did not deserve to be called readers – no indeed, consumers, that was all they were. And Boncassa would hold forth about how the work he himself was engaged upon, day in day out, year in year out, transcended the old weaknesses and opportunism of writers past and present . . . a never-ending opus, a phenomenal undertaking – unpublishable, of course, but it was literature, dammit, literature!

Madame Pélagie would hang around as long as she could until Vollard pushed open the glass door at last, tight-lipped and exhausted. Then she would quickly put on her little black coat, light up, seize her bag laden with books and disappear into the night. Lately she had noticed Vollard looking at the books with what she called "hospital eyes", and she had no doubt that he took his husky "book voice" with him to the hospital every day.

Then came that wintry morning when the sky was a stunning blue and the shrill light penetrated the recesses of a certain room. As though possessed by his own words, Vollard let his voice do the talking, making its way as usual into the labyrinth of unlikely hearing. But on that day the voice slowed down, faltered and stammered as though approaching a secret chamber. Suddenly, while his voice floundered on, Vollard noticed that the child's eyes were wide open: the big black eyes were not looking at anything in particular, but they were "looking". He held his face up close to the awesome, wide-eyed look. A look that had burst open, like a wound, or an undiscovered flower.

The flutter of eyelids. An infinitesimal movement of the pupils. And finally the faintest of twitchings at the corners of eyes and lips. The plaster mask banished by a hint of awareness. But Vollard could not stop now, not in the middle of the very beautiful passage, very simple, and perhaps magical, that he was telling: *"And the moment came . . . when something unique . . . something that will never happen again in this way, a sensation of such force, that even now, after so much time . . ."*

He continued without pausing for breath, persuaded that certain words – but which ones? *Petals . . . trembling . . . lattice . . . waves of life?* – had the incredible power of animating the inanimate, of rousing a soul even as a petal or a wave.

The child's eyes, having closed several times, now stayed open. As if, behind them, there was vision, the effort to understand, the will to return. *"Fledgling swallow on a cornice!"*

Yes, the hint was there. Not consciousness as yet, but a very fragile capacity for awareness. Not yet a child named Éva, but a sense of childhood, a youthful presence humbly welcomed by Vollard.

The news was quick to spread. Presently there were nurses gathering round, hovering over the child's bed to witness the signs of return, the "miracle of awakening".

Thérèse arrived in the middle of the excitement. Unaccustomed to anything but flying visits, she was unsure at first how to react when they drew back for her to embrace the little girl. She kissed her on the cheek and said in a dull, halting voice: "I'm here, Éva, your maman's here . . ." Then she anxiously lifted her eyes, as though seeking reassurance for her conduct from the looks fixed on her. On her lips, the words were not so much convincing as listless, but the nurses were touched all the same. She did her best, Thérèse did, and the following days she forced herself to spend more time at the hospital with Éva.

She took off her coat, pushed up her sleeves and took up station by the bed. She smiled and touched the cheeks of the child, who was beginning to stir, moving her head from side to side, following the movements in the room with her eyes, opening her mouth, but not saying anything. Vollard, accustomed over time to being alone with the child in a silence that was only broken by his own voice, was equally unsure how to behave. He withdrew to the corridor so as not to be in her way. He stood there for a time, observing the scene. His eyes met Thérèse's more than once, but finding that she had nothing to say either, he turned and strode away.

They explained to Thérèse: "Your little girl has finally emerged from the coma. Stay with her. Stimulate her with detailed descriptions of memories you share, happy memories. She has to find her bearings, learn to recognise people and things . . ."

Thérèse was seized with panic. She could not think of any really happy memory to share. What was she supposed to describe? Some long drive through a desolate landscape? Hanging around in some dismal suburb? Being reunited after some delay? The hotels they stayed at . . . hotels invariably called "De la Gare", "Du Commerce", "Des Voyageurs". Same smell of carpets. Same tarnished mirrors.

"Éva, remember that room at the back of the restaurant where the two of us used to sleep, on mattresses we'd put down after my shift when everyone had left, and where it smelled of soup and stale tobacco?" Or: "And that lovely villa where a very kind and very widowed old gent put us up, the two of us, during that winter? Big quiet rooms, an open fire. The old man talked about his dead wife the whole time; in the end he took me for her. You, you were still tiny. You were a baby, you cried at night, which got on the old man's nerves. He'd never had children. He kept complaining, and one day I grabbed your Moses basket and off we went."

Vague images straggled across Thérèse's memory, but she was struck dumb in the face of her mute child.

Éva Blanchot's case was of passing interest to the doctors, who bustled into the room, gravely consulted the case notes, summarily examined the patient, then vanished. During those early days the nurses would enter the room in cheerful mood, addressing Éva in loud voices: "Good morning, Éva! And how are you this morning?"

Éva seemed to follow their movements with her eyes, which widened momentarily, then went blank.

Soon the bright expressions began to cloud. The whispering resumed. The doctor cleared his throat and shook his head. Éva looked around dreamily, moving an arm or a finger when asked to do so. She understood everything, it seemed, but her responses were weak.

The diagnosis was delivered: "Well, Madame Blanchot, your daughter will live. Her organs will heal. Her fractures are mending very satisfactorily. Unfortunately . . . certain injuries appear to be irreversible. There may be some lasting damage . . ."

The doctor had drawn Thérèse into a quiet office. All she had eyes for was his dandruff, his furrowed brow, his hands performing a comic dance that jarred with the solemn tone and low voice.

"My dear Madame Blanchot, medical science lets us down more often than we like to admit. Your daughter has won a victory, but she has also suffered defeat . . . Each case is unique, complex, mysterious. Your friend — well, the gentleman — has, I am told, shown remarkable dedication. But she will not regain all her faculties . . ."

Thérèse understood instinctively that she was supposed to ask questions. She opened her mouth to speak, but the doctor cut her short.

"No, you'll see, she'll regain movement, she'll learn to walk again. With rehabilitation therapy, it may all go quite quickly, but . . ."

"But what?"

"Éva has lost the power of speech! Still, you'll be able to communicate with her, I'm sure. She'll understand some things, and she'll be able to make herself understood a little, but she won't be able to talk. The damage to the language centre is irreversible, although, as with everything else, one can't be absolutely sure . . . But I would prefer . . . it is important to prepare yourself, to come to terms with . . . a handicapped child."

Numbed, Thérèse heard the words resonate: handicapped, mother of a handicapped child, a mother handicapped by a little girl . . . Éva at her side for ever. Not talking, just sticking to her. They'd be stuck in the same place all the time!

The doctor with the furrowed brow droned on.

"That is why specialised care offers a good solution. There are several rehabilitation centres around here, in the Chartreuse. Just half an hour by car. You can go and see her often."

Saying yes, yes . . . Thérèse was desperate for the interview to end. She shifted forward on her chair, rose to her feet and backed away towards the door. The last she heard was: "There is always room for hope. Keep hoping. Each body is an enigma unto itself. The enigma of the body."

In the hallway, alone at last, she thought of something to write in the notebook she kept for jotting down thoughts. She would use big letters to write: "Each body an enigma unto itself. The enigma of the body." Then it slipped her mind.

Not long afterwards Éva was well enough to leave the hospital. Wearing her new clothes, she was like any other dark-eyed little girl in a black down parka. But she had to be helped to the ambulance, carried like a doll. Pale skin and scars still visible. Frail-looking. Wide forehead. Genderless perplexity. Ageless sorrow.

Her gaze was fleeting. One moment she would seem to be looking at something in the distance, the next she would be staring at some insignificant detail, a pearl button or a strand of wool, a pink postmark, a crumb, the condensation on a window pane . . . without making a sound. She said nothing at all, and did not appear to want to either. She responded to some requests, took hold of objects that were handed to her, handed them back, too; she could feed herself, and it was not long before she was taking small steps without any assistance.

Once she had settled in at the rehabilitation centre on the mountain, the staff had reason to be pleased. She walked long stretches in the hallways and even in the park. With the air of a tightrope walker, thin little arms spread out for balance, alone, very alone, and mute.

The speech therapists, however, were disappointed, for they failed to coax the least sound from her, not even a grunt or a whisper. No utterance of any kind. Just silence. Unlike the other patients, who were always cautious and apprehensive, Éva propelled herself resolutely forward, and soon she was quite fast, going in any direction without the least fear of stumbling or losing her balance. It was not boldness on her part, it was a kind of ghostly indifference. They had to go after her, make her stop. Then she would stand stock-still, stonily confronting the majestic sweep of the mountains opposite the terrace of the rehabilitation centre.

Bookseller Vollard had not been to see Éva again. Had not wished to. Once her emergence from coma was definitive, he holed up in "The Verb To Be", spending all his time reading, sorting books, picking up the thread of past conversations with regular clients, putting up with

Boncassa's tirades in the late afternoon. He had telephoned for news about the little girl. He was aware of the prognosis. Regained mobility. But speech impaired. Inexistence.

During his sleepless nights the battle between the "anguished voice" and the sentences from books started up again. Not that he minded. Right now, Vollard wanted to forget the child. Forget the accident. Read, read, and forget. Forget the final terror-stricken look. Forget the sound of a body being cracked. Forget the plaster mask. Forget the slew of texts recited in the maze of the absence. He had recalled so many books, recited so many stories. He was worn out, slumped at his desk, head bowed.

"You shall recite in the name of him who created you from a crust of dried blood! You shall recite in the name of him who created you from a gobbet of spittle! You shall recite in the name of him who created you from an ink spot! You shall read and you shall recite . . . ."

Vollard wanted nothing more than to ensconce himself at the heart of his large web, surrounded and shielded by books.

That was not reckoning on a visit from Thérèse Blanchot. He was unprepared for this surprise encounter in the late spring. She had pushed open the glazed door of "The Verb To Be" one fateful afternoon of icy draughts in the shadowy back streets and brooding warmth in the sunlit squares. What had she come for? She had had a moment's hesitation reaching for the book-shaped door handle, then she had stepped inside. Madame Pélagie was the only person there, in the back. She told the young woman she did not know where Vollard was. Crestfallen, Thérèse turned to go. She made her way towards the exit very slowly, not paying the slightest heed to the books on display and in piles all around.

"Monsieur Vollard won't be long," Madame Pélagie said, lighting a cigarette. Smoke poured from her nostrils.

Invited to wait for his return, Thérèse hesitated again. Then she too lit up, and posted herself by the glazed door. An hour went by, then another. Madame Pélagie showed no surprise, asked no questions. She understood.

Not even to kill time, not even to foil her impatience, did Thérèse so much as glance at the books. She seemed oblivious to their existence. No deciphering of titles, no finger absently touching a cover, no skimming of pages at random.

She stood by the door and waited, making a vague gesture towards the street from time to time and then changing her mind, half watching the people in the square outside while new customers came in and others left with their purchases, obliging her to draw back a little each time.

Thérèse held her big, heavy shopping bag close to her chest. Amongst a jumble of musty-smelling odds and ends it contained her spiral notebook. Suddenly, she dug her hand in and fished the notebook out. It showed signs of wear and tear. She could not decide whether to open it, so she contented herself with hugging it like a talisman, a pathetic shield scrawled with magical phrases. Across one page she had written "Enigma of bodies. Each body its own enigma". But there were longer entries, too, scribbled at all angles, phrases lifted from here, from there: "Each person's misery a drop in the ocean. Each drop an ocean in itself." And: "Envying everyone who sinks into gloom. It's too gloomy to see them sink . . . SAD AND OF NO IMPORTANCE."

After a while Thérèse slipped the notebook back into her bag. She went on waiting.

Coming in through the back door, Vollard immediately recognised the slight figure of the young woman, whom he seemed to be peering at through the wrong end of a telescope. Thérèse seen from behind. Thérèse against the light, the way he had seen her the first time.

A few heavy strides and he was behind her. She spun round, almost colliding with him, then steadied herself. She seemed to have forgotten why she had come. The bookseller did nothing to put her at ease. Huge frame, dangling arms, expectant.

"Éva?"

Thérèse hastened to tell him the news:

"A specialised centre. Yes, still there, she'll be there for a long time yet. Still hasn't said a single word. Very sweet, though. Meek. Disconcerting. Very frail, too. Eats hardly anything. She brings the food to her lips, keeps it in her mouth, waits for someone to tell her to swallow. She faints sometimes, which is what the doctor said might happen. She may be in pain, too, when her face goes all tense and her body all stiff. But things are getting better, they're getting better. She comes when you call her. She walks in the park. She enjoys looking at things, picking stuff up from the ground. They're looking after her. She's well cared for."

"I know. What did you want to see me about?"

Vollard cleared his throat noisily.

Thérèse made a wry face, paused, and then told him why she had come. She explained that she couldn't keep going to the specialised centre every day, or even very often at all. Besides, she had just found a job miles away. Nowhere near the Chartreuse. A more or less steady job, reasonable wages, but really very far away. She had practically no money left. So it was back to the old routine: sales assistant, waitress, checkout girl. Well, a bar would have been nice, what with day shifts and night shifts, serving drinks . . .

"You do understand, don't you, Monsieur Vollard? I couldn't help thinking of you. I said to myself: you never can tell, seeing as how you're the only person she knows around here, having spent so much time with her . . . you know? A visit from time to time. If you have a spare moment, I don't know, on a Sunday or so . . . Yesterday when I was up there I wrote a letter, I signed forms, I gave them your name. It's all official. It's all right for you to go and see her, take her for walks. Know what I mean? I'd better be off now. I'm starting tomorrow . . ."

Distraught, Vollard rubbed his hands together, kneading the base of each thumb.

Suddenly, without thinking, Thérèse reached up to the bookseller's fists, joined like a solid, bony bundle bristling with ginger hairs, and covered them with her own small hands, spreading her fingers as though clinging to a lichen-covered rock. Vollard did not object. With men, Thérèse was capable of being direct in this way. Her directness was all the easier for her basically not giving a damn. Since her precocious emergence from childhood, Thérèse had known that with men she could afford to behave pretty much any way she liked. But as to what she liked, she had no idea at all.

Holding tight to these strange hands, the young woman told him in short bursts how to get to the rehabilitation centre, in case he had forgotten where Éva was staying. She explained where the new shopping mall was, miles away, where she would be working from now on, as a sales assistant, waitress or checkout girl.

Vollard felt the pressure of Thérèse's delicate fingers on his hands, but he kept very still, as still as when a summer butterfly alights an instant on one's shoulder or cheek. Summer was coming. The butterfly would be off.

The Grande Chartreuse

Like all things massive, the Massif de la Chartreuse harbours a plethora of folds, creases, furrows, pleats, variously seen as enticing or repellent. One would think the silvered, fluted rock inhabited by an enigmatic soul. For while the peaceable imagery is present – pine trees, grassy vales, grey cliffs, calcareous crags, torrents, combes and pastures – one very quickly suspects some greater force at work, as if a giant's hand had scrunched the earth's crust into a geological complex that lends itself to the burying of thoughts, to the secreting of bodies, and a distancing from the world within reach of the sky.

For century upon century, at the secret heart of this heart of rock, has beaten a Gregorian pulse, muted and crystalline by turns. The distant chime of bells, like the waves of a great solitude, rolling from one summit to the next, across faults and fissures. Unlike some mountain ranges, the Chartreuse is not easy of access. It is something of a multi-layered labyrinth, because all the peaks, hollows and ridges that appear in close proximity on the map are in fact great distances apart.

It was in the Chartreuse that Vollard would go walking, often to the point of exhaustion. He would talk to himself as he walked, wearing himself out walking and talking.

Towards evening, when the curvature of space becomes the curvature of time, when the trees cast lengthening shadows on meadows decked with St John's wort and thistle and the forest of black pine forms a sharp angle with a field yet inundated with light, Vollard would drop to the ground amid the tall grasses and spills of shale, the smell of earth and bark, and there, at last, he would open a book, any book, with sentences that were as likely to be in complete harmony as at odds with the surroundings.

Two weeks had gone by since Thérèse's visit to "The Verb To Be". Vollard had not been up in the mountains since the accident, nor had he felt any inclination to pay the little girl a visit, as her mother had so urgently requested. But driving his van one Sunday morning in May, he realised that he was on the winding road that led up to the village near the rehabilitation centre. He did not know what had made him take this direction, for he was not planning to go and see the child. He was driving slowly on the narrow road through the forest. He would not go all the way there, he decided. He would just take a look at the place where the little girl would from now on be living.

The rehabilitation centre stood among other medical facilities just above the village, on a narrow mountain ridge sheltered from the north wind by a long bluff and forests of oak and spruce. A secluded, shielded place. Time was when those buildings were sanatoriums. A time of hacking coughs, fevers and expectorations in the pure air of the magic mountain. But nowadays, in the valleys down below, coughing no longer killed. The sanatoriums fell into disuse. Nowadays, in the valleys down below, it was car crashes that killed. Bodies were savaged and broken in road accidents. Paralysis, trauma, hemiplegia, amputations. Booksellers ran over little girls.

Vollard parked his van in the village square, slipped a couple of books into a bag just in case and set off on foot in the direction of the imposing buildings of the medical centre. Thérèse's description was enough for him to locate the block where Éva – traumatised, speechless, but having recovered the use of her limbs – was now living, in abeyance. On the way there he passed a little shoal of wheelchairs occupied by youthful patients with wasted legs, skinny arms and neck-braces. They were being pushed by other youngsters, hale and hearty and chatting away among themselves.

He hesitated, then started across a grassy park-like area towards a vast terrace overlooking the valley. There, in the open air, another scattering of crippled, mangled youngsters, in addition to some older men with crutches and artificial limbs. Vollard kept walking. The bag weighed down with books thudded against his hip. He passed a man with long white hair making his way painfully slowly with the aid of a walking-frame. More wheelchairs.

Seeing the small figure poised motionless by the grey stone boundary, staring out across the valley at the dramatic barrier of snow-capped mountains, Vollard knew at once it was Éva. He recognised her, even from behind, the way one recognises one's mother. Her hair had grown. Standing perfectly still, arms hanging at her sides, her gaze lost in the distance, in the snowy heights, the blue. There was a slight breeze, and when Éva tilted her head a fraction her dark fringe lifted in the cool air.

Once he had glimpsed her face, not even sad-looking, but vacant, unbearably remote, Vollard knew that he had gone too far, that what he had seen was beyond him, and the idea of their eyes meeting again filled him with panic. What good would it do anyway? She was being looked after. Alive. Turned to stone.

Anything he might still do or say would be in vain. Vanity of vanities.

Vollard doubled back across the grounds and returned to the village, where the sun blazed on pinky-grey roofs and yellow walls festooned with mature wisterias. It seemed a good place to linger awhile. By himself, in the unwitting tepidity of things, on this mountain ledge so difficult of access. The noon hour rang out. The echoes took for ever to die away. Sporty, sturdily shod types of all ages lined up their rucksacks along a stone wall and installed themselves in the open-air cafés. Feeling hungry and thirsty himself, Vollard too moved to one of the wooden tables set out on the square with a view of the vast landscape. Reaching automatically in his bag, he drew out a book at random, which he placed on the table in front of him. "*Everywhere I looked for peace of mind, I never found it but in a corner with a book.*"

Food, drink, and a book amid the buzz of conversation

and clink of glasses. General anaesthetic. Sun-struck froth on his beer. A sense of cosmic indifference, which was both harrowing and in some way reassuring.

Later he was back at the wheel, driving very slowly. Shoulders hunched, elbow out of the open window, fresh air on his face. He had polished the thick lenses of his glasses yet again, but his perception of everything, mountains, forests, villages, meadows, roads, was vague and misty. As always, whole sentences came into his mind, which contributed to keeping the scenery at a distance.

The views were splendid. The road snaked steadily upwards, following the curves of the mountain. The late spring light softened the tall grasses and the budding leaves on the trees. Everything dissolved into swathes of golden vapour and hazy shadows tinged with blue. A world wreathed in the enigmatic smile of a limitless deity, a god all too happy to have forsaken his creation and all the creatures in it.

Suddenly Étienne Vollard's eyes lit upon a vast stretch of water, green and deep. An artificial lake, flat as a sheet of iron, with steeply rising slopes. Almost supernaturally tranquil, the high mountain lake narrowed at one end towards a gorge, where it poured in a great roaring torrent on to bare rocks and down into the valley beyond, way below.

Then he saw the bridge, a skeletal arch spanning the entrance to the gorge. As he drew nearer, driving increasingly slowly, he could make out small coloured shapes on the bridge. He stopped his van some way off and continued on foot. The dusty road was practically deserted; here and there small rocks had become detached from the mountainside. Vollard walked on in the silence, in the smell of earth. The bridge was close by. Suddenly a long-drawn-out shriek was heard, thrown back by the echo. A huge cry, a scream of delighted terror, of triumphant exhilaration. Someone had jumped. The echo also bounced back some applause, then more shouts, of sheer joy this time, and jubilation.

Vollard started across the bridge, in the middle of which a young crowd had gathered. A sign said: EUROPEAN BUNGY-JUMP CENTRE: DIVES OF 108 METRES! And beneath, in fluorescent letters: EXPERIENCE THE THRILL OF VERTIGO, and a clumsily drawn half-bird half-human. A man stood by the parapet calmly operating the motorised winch to raise the jumper who was even now dangling at the end of the rope. Vollard leaned over and watched the graceful ascent of a youthful body hanging on to the elastic with only one hand. The free hand, gloved in yellow, blew kisses to the cluster of friends waiting on the bridge, leaning out over the abyss with the torrent boiling in its depths.

It was a girl in a bright red jumpsuit. She clambered on to the parapet, laughed and lifted off her helmet, likewise red, releasing a cascade of blonde hair down her neck and shoulders. Boys extended arms and hands to help her down. She kissed several of them. They were a tightly knit gang. Kitted out in their sports gear they radiated a brazen capacity for enjoyment – of reality, of material things, of the light. Vollard watched from a discreet distance, elbows propped on the balustrade. The next one to jump was already waiting on the edge of the drop, a distant look in his eyes. Concentrated, helmeted, gloved. Arms spread out wide. Feet together, bindings firmly secured around his ankles. There was a hush of expectation. He inhaled hard and then, with a great shout, hurled himself into the deep, plummeting down to the moist shadows of the abyss as if he would fall to his death on the gleaming rocks below.

But, sure enough, at the last moment the elastic gave and stretched and gave, curbing the free fall, braking the impetus more and more until a precisely calculated length had been achieved, and at that point the jumper, instead of hitting the ground, was catapulted skyward, the long cord rippling limply in his wake.

The body dropped again. Bounced up again. A giant pendulum. A human yo-yo, shouting with increasing elation. Vollard's heart was thumping, rising to his throat with that familiar mix of nausea and trepidation. He moved closer to the group, the better to study the face of the one on his way up. Meanwhile the blonde girl stripped off her jumpsuit, her lovely bare shoulders emerged from the scarlet fabric, long tanned arms, gestures of a casual, natural ease.

"What have they got that I haven't? Why can they jump like that? Live the way they jump? Breathe, talk, look at things with such matter-of-factness?"

Three men and two women in garish figure-hugging outfits

took turns jumping off the bridge. The winch operator's eyes shifted to Vollard. Several youngsters gave him curious looks.

"Can anyone take a jump like this?" Vollard inquired in a blank, almost hoarse voice. He cleared his throat and repeated: "Can anyone?"

"Of course, monsieur, everybody can jump. They've just got to overcome their fear. Fear of the void. Unless they have a heart condition, of course. But there's no risk involved. It's all calculated."

Clearing his throat again, Vollard adjusted his glasses. He heard himself say:

"What does it cost? How much to have a go? Could I do it today? Do you have to book ahead?"

Several people were listening. The winch operator said, with sincere astonishment: "Is it for *yourself* you're asking?" while he looked Vollard up and down as though gauging his weight.

No, not for me, for a friend, a young chap, Vollard was going to say, but his voice came out with: "Yes, for me, I'd like to try. Is that possible?"

The winch operator was a fair bit shorter than Vollard. Stocky build, lined face, calm. The beginnings of a smile froze on his lips as if he suddenly became aware of something momentous going on, something that was beyond his scope. In the even, unruffled tones of the experienced mountaineer, all he said was:

"Sure, no problem. If you want to try, that's fine. In a little while, when everyone on the list has had their turn."

But Vollard had the impression that the smirk which the man had succeeded in wiping off his face had passed to the lips of the young bystanders. He felt himself squirming in the absurdity of it all. Far from home, far from his books, and from the bookshop. Alone in the company of these muscular angels with their bright plumage. Human beings that were too beautiful, too real.

Soon they were crowding round him, helping him into the harness as best they could, fastening the leather straps round his ankles. No-one was laughing, but the absence of laughter made it worse. Had he been less scared, Vollard would have been moved by their zealous attentions, by their pretending not to be in the least surprised that a middle-aged bloke wearing outsize grey trousers and an outsize white shirt with sweat stains should wish to leap off this bridge.

"Better take off your glasses before you jump, don't you think?"

The blonde girl offered to hold his jacket for him.

"We'll lend you one of our helmets, don't you worry. And gloves."

The light was brilliant. A few more cars had parked along the ramp to the bridge. People had come to gawp, some of them armed with cameras. There was nothing to stop them watching and filming this man in his preposterous harness. This monumental, vulnerable creature. Fish out of water. At the very last moment, in an effort to exorcise his mounting, paralysing panic, he blurted the question concerning his own weight.

"Too heavy? Not at all, nothing to worry about," he was told. "The elasticity is calculated for weights of up to a hundred and fifty kilos."

They guide his foot on to the little stepladder. Next tread. And the next. He hears the purr of a camcorder. Someone is filming him. He draws himself upright on the parapet. On the edge of the precipice. The small crowd lapses into silence. His heart pounds. He feels faint from nausea. What is he doing there? Towering over his humble retinue, he could launch into any recitation he pleased, right there in front of them all. Reel it off from memory. Calm would be restored. Reciting would prevent him losing consciousness.

He surveys the black pool. The crags. One hundred and eight metres of drop. He has time to remember that he has never dived in his life, not even as a boy in the chlorinated swimming pools of his schooldays. Not ever in the sea, either.

Behind him, a voice breaks the deathly silence: "Go for it!" His arms are pinned to his thighs. The bridge is bathed in sunshine, but Vollard shivers. Voices murmur: "Whenever you're ready . . ."

Uppermost in Vollard's mind is the fear of his legs giving way beneath him, so that instead of jumping he will tumble helplessly into the awesome hole. Words of encouragement come from the waiting crowd, a first quip, then a sarcastic remark.

He stands there wishing he could call the whole thing off. Get away. Free himself from this entanglement. Finally he

[130]

hears someone say: "Oh well, it can happen to anyone. Stage fright. Don't force yourself." A hideous deliverance: the same "these things happen . . ." of all fiascos. The humiliating defeat experienced by all who find themselves incapable of rising to a lunatic and absurd challenge and have only themselves to blame.

"Well, sir, these things happen, you know . . . Don't force yourself. We'll get you down."

At that point Vollard gives up. He wavers on the stepladder. The next candidate in line grows impatient, gives him a little nudge. Vollard would like to hear them laugh. But no, there is no laughter, nor jeering. His glasses are returned to him. The blonde girl hands him his jacket absent-mindedly. He moves away, across the bridge, and no-one watches him as he goes. He is in urgent need of something to eat, to fill his mouth, his stomach, his head. At the end of the bridge there is a van with refreshments. Vollard buys a pizza and some beer. The froth runs down his beard. He starts down the road, but despite his desire to get away he slumps down against a rock in the verge, in the shade of the fir trees.

He can only think of sinking into defeat, a void that he will never be able to span. Little by little Vollard grows calm.

Seated at the base of his rock, unnoticed by anyone, the phrases started up again. Where did they come from, those accursed, all too familiar phrases? From what abyss did they arise? " . . . *the sorriest struggle you can imagine. Taking place in a fathomless gloom, nothing underfoot, nothing around you, no*

witnesses, no cheering, no glory, no burning desire for victory, no
great dread of defeat either."

As the afternoon drew to a close the sun dipped behind the peaks soaring above the lake. The bridge suspended over the gorge was devoured by the advancing shadows. The crowd of bungy-jumpers had thinned. They hung about, chatting and drinking.

It was a time for sharing emotions, for exulting in conquered terrors. A time for reliving other, no less intrepid experiences, in the mountains, on the ice, in the snow, ascending the dizzying heights of glaciers, diving in faraway oceans. The youngsters sat on their heels around the winch, which had been switched off. The distant roar of the torrent could be heard, and from time to time the shrill cry of a bird of prey gliding upwards in the fading light. The sightseers had long since left. It was very quiet in the gathering dusk. Yet another dusk.

No-one questioned the motives people might have for making these extreme plunges into space. Were they trying to prove something? Obviously the proof would be self-defeating. Proof of what, anyway?

No indeed, these youngsters were lovers of the moment, friends of the here and now. Their bodies were exactly right for where they stood in the world. Instantly attuned to one another. That was the way things were. Girls and boys laughing and chatting, quietly at ease in each other's company.

The winch operator started gathering up his equipment.

The pizza vendor had gone. Gradually the youngsters made ready to leave. That was when they saw the burly figure they had forgotten about heading in their direction again. He was carrying his grey jacket over his arm, his shirt was tucked into his trousers, and he was smiling ruefully. Acting quickly now, he laid his jacket on the parapet and declared that he was ready for the harness and helmet. He grabbed a pair of leather gloves, which he drew on with the air of a boxer before a fight. He handed his glasses to the blonde girl.

He gave off a fierce determination, a ferocity for which the youngsters were unprepared, a fury which they could not take in, although they obliged him almost mechanically. The silence was heavy. The sun had gone. Cries from birds of prey, the rush of water. Hardly had the straps been fastened when Vollard clambered on to the parapet, and without waiting for a signal, without striking the bungy-jumper's pose, he flung himself heavily, clumsily, into the void, twisting as he dropped, his arms flailing, shirt tails billowing like ineffectual wings. This was no leap of an angel, it was a dead-weight fall. Vollard plummeted down until the giant fist tightened its grip on his ankles, curbing his speed, while the ravine loomed up, enveloping him in an icy cold.

When the elastic was stretched to its limit Vollard felt his body being yanked skyward, as if his hundred and ten kilos were suddenly immaterial. The sensation of being suspended in an eternity of distress, losing track of whether he was going up or down, still rising or already tumbling again, yet another descent, another rebound, on and on.

Little by little the momentum died away. The ridiculous yo-yo came to rest, completely unwound and dangling, but the huge body still swung to and fro like a pendulum over the glistening humps of rock. Vollard tried frantically to turn and twist the way he had seen the other divers do, but he did not manage to take hold of the cord attached to his ankles, nor was he able to haul himself upright along a metre or two of the sling. He just hung there by his feet with his head fifteen metres off the ground, waiting for the winch to be set in motion for his motorised ascent.

He had trouble breathing normally. There was vomit in his nostrils, in his eyes and in his hair. For he had vomited a little, thrown up some of the contents of this failed Oedipus, without either destiny or complex, dangling at the end of a thick umbilical cord made of rubber. But he could feel that the words from all his books were still firmly in place in his skull.

He was hoisted up to safety. Support was offered, and help with cleaning himself up, tucking in his shirt, putting on his jacket and his glasses. Not a word was said. No-one had the slightest desire to laugh. The organisers tidied away the bungy-jumping paraphernalia, as Vollard, unsteadily, headed off the bridge to the road where he had left his van.

Having squeezed himself behind the wheel, ankles hurting, temples throbbing, he was overcome by his own stench. His shirt and trousers were drenched with sweat. There were still traces of sick in his hair and in his beard. His glasses were filthy. "I stink. Right now I stink," he told himself. And he sensed that over and above the vomit and the sweat there was the stench of dread, that strange odour of corpses and reeking sap which, in the end, is all-pervading.

La petite Chartreuse

His mind made up, Vollard drove directly to the rehabilitation centre the following Sunday. He called on the deputy director, who gave a yawn wide enough to dislocate his jaw as he rummaged around in his minute, cluttered office to find Thérèse Blanchot's note authorising one "Monsieur Vollard (Étienne), bookseller by trade" to visit little Éva, whose rehabilitation was proving so arduous.

Vollard was surprised he was not asked for identification, but he followed the deputy director down the corridors without comment.

"We were hoping for a visit from you, I have to say, Monsieur Vollard. You are her uncle? A relative? Ah well, that is no concern of mine! But it is good for the little girl to have visitors. Her mother has had to take a job far away from here, I believe . . . She only came a few times, and spent very little time here when she did. The child is doing all right, although there has been no actual progress to speak of. There seems to be some irreversible damage. She has not yet spoken at all."

They made their way into a large room where young victims of the most horrendous accidents were playing cards, in their wheelchairs, their torsos encased in stiff corsets, chins supported by braces. From a television set poured a thick sauce of gaudy inanities. Several handicapped youngsters, their voices weirdly thick or staccato from twisted mouths, swore at each other over a packet of cigarettes, arms distorted, flying theatrically, acting tough.

Éva was sitting right under the shelf with the television set, indifferent to the tobacco smoke and the tumult. Dreamy and vague. Observing her, Vollard was for some reason reminded of a film projector, whirring and clicking and giving off a beam of warm light, but having no reel with images.

He squatted down as best he could beside the calm, frail-looking child. He held out a huge upturned palm, but the little girl did not react. And yet – she did look at the proffered hand, and it was possible to imagine a glint of irony at the back of her dark-ringed eyes. Gently, Vollard took hold of Éva's hand, as if it were the paw of a small animal, a cross between a frog and a sparrow or between a grasshopper and a ferret, and laid it on his palm. By degrees, the two disproportionate hands clasped one another. Vollard cupped his hand very slightly, and the little girl's fingers, too, began to stir in token of their willingness to curl up on this warm pad creased with the lines of life, adversity and the heart.

"By all means take her out for a walk! Of course! She does take part in the group outings, but no-one has taken her out on her own for a walk along the footpaths around here. Her mother seldom has time. But Éva's legs are in good shape."

Vollard and Éva left the building together. He stooped a little to hold hands with the child, who allowed herself to be led along, saying not a word. Presently they were out in the countryside on a track that led nowhere in particular . . . It was impossible to say whether the child was aware of the mountain scenery, or indeed if she was conscious of her surroundings at all, but there did seem to be a glimmer of recognition, what with her hard breathing, flared nostrils, and the way she shut her eyes now and then as though sensing the weight of the chill air on her lids.

Vollard had to curb his normal large strides. He forced himself to adjust his pace to the feather-light steps of his companion, whose meekness gave an illusion of trust. They strolled through a scattering of oak trees on a footpath flanked by tall grasses and rocky crags, then among the serried ranks of spruce. The bookseller kept an anxious eye on the trodden path for any jutting roots and stones, tightening his hold on the small hand wrapped in his while Éva walked on without ever stumbling. Between the tree trunks there were fleeting glimpses of the rehabilitation centre down below.

As the track was rising too steeply, Vollard decided to turn off into a meadow. He had no particular destination in mind, just wanted the child to have the chance of a real airing. He had the sensation that the Grande Chartreuse was going to close in on them like a gigantic hand. All was in suspense in this freshness, this intoxicating mountain air.

They came to a large clearing carpeted in thick, springy grass. Huge stone chunks fallen from the mountain, now fleeced in orange lichen, seemed to be a huddle of prehistoric beasts burrowing their snouts in the ground.

It was there that Vollard thought of letting go of the little girl's hand, of setting her free with the gentlest of encouragements that she walk by herself in the bright light. That she take some steps all on her own. Maybe put on a little speed. And, who knows, spring about and frolic like an animal let off the rein or leash.

But Éva unhurriedly planted her hand back into Vollard's and stared into space, waiting for him to start walking again. Which he did, slowly, using his free hand in passing to feel the roughness of the rocks fallen there for centuries.

He returned three days later. This time Éva and he wended their unsteady way to another meadow, and to a swift, clear mountain stream which dissected it. Patiently, he coaxed Éva to kneel down on the moss. There was a strong smell of earth and soaking wood. The stones at the water's edge were wet and slippery. Some of them rolled about underfoot. Vollard stepped into the riverbed in his big shoes, wetting the bottoms of his trousers. He scooped some water with his hands and offered his brimming cup to Éva.

He waited as the water trickled between his fingers, and before long the little girl reached out to touch, tapping very lightly at first and then making little splashes that sparkled in the sunshine. When there was no water left, Vollard started anew. She grew tired. She switched off.

Then he handed her a wet pebble, which she held against her cheek until Vollard took her arm and helped her to cast it in a pool. He did the same with a second pebble, gently guiding the thin little arm, inviting the fingers to let it go.

Éva's dark eyes seemed to register the successive "plops" with faint pleasure. Despite her silence and the blankness of her expression, Vollard believed he detected a childish satisfaction, born of an inaccessible, featureless childhood. He even felt himself the tingle of a very ancient yet immediate joy. Casting a pebble into the water. Taking aim and throwing. Making splashes. Ripples widening in the water. Under Éva's eyes, he took to throwing bigger and bigger stones to make bigger and bigger splashes.

Éva remained quite still, open-mouthed, her arm held slightly forward. She did not smile, but Vollard fancied that the glimmer of sadness in the depths of her pupils had softened a little.

A few days went by. Vollard drove up to the rehabilitation centre again. And several more times. Éva tired very easily; the stream was as far as she could walk. Vollard even had the impression that she was drawn to that place. One time, he undid the straps of her sandals so that she might paddle barefoot in the cold stream, leaning on him for support. He helped her on to stepping-stones which rumbled hollowly underfoot, and then into mid-stream, up to her ankles in the lacy foam.

Finally he lifted her up, wiped her feet with his jacket and sat her down on the moss. All about them was silent. From the wood close by came the drill of a woodpecker, the snapping of a branch. During these walks Vollard spoke very little. His tongue was almost as tied as hers. He concentrated on taking small steps. He thought up a thousand little sensations for her to experience. One day, after yet another paddle in the stream, Vollard drew himself upright, cleared his throat and, jacking his knees up high with each step, began to declaim with comical gravity: "*One day, no matter when or where, a long-legged heron chanced to fare . . .*'"

Éva was sitting on a stone with Vollard's jacket tucked round her legs for warmth. She seemed to be watching and listening as he lingered over the words, letting them resonate in the stillness: "*By a certain river's brink : . . the water was clear and still, the carp and the pike there at will . . .*'

The bookseller affected the disdain of a heron. High-stepping, craning his neck. His shoes were filled with water. He repeated: "*Clear and still!*' and swooped down to put his hands into the current, swimming like a carp or pike. He drew out the "*looong sharp beak . . . looong and sharp*". Then, just as he was giving his dramatic rendition of "*So near came the scaly fry they might be caught by the passer-by*", he noticed that Éva was trembling. Pallid face. Sunken, glittering eyes. He took fright. He bundled the child up in his jacket, so that he could see only the small, surprised face, gathered her in his arms and strode down the path to the rehabilitation centre.

How many more times did he take Éva on an outing of some sort or another among the folds of the Grande Chartreuse? Did she look forward to his visits? Did she enjoy their escapades?

He led her to wild bowers, among tree trunks of green velvet and ridges of rock and low-hanging branches. But Éva became tired more and more quickly. Her interest never now seemed to be aroused. On several occasions she had seemed to want to throw pebbles into the water by herself. She had seemed to enjoy paddling in the stream. But she was as remote as ever. Noting her exhaustion, Vollard would tighten his hold on her, but when her legs buckled he would lift her into his arms and then on to his shoulders, pointing out a tree, a mountain peak, now and then a cloud, or raising his finger to alert her to the call of a woodpecker close by.

They went for drives in his van, stopping in some village to buy her pain au chocolat, raisin pastries, sweet-smelling baguettes, but Éva scarcely tasted them. She could barely walk unaided any more.

When he put her on his shoulders he thought how light she was, far too light at any rate, and he would steady her with his hands until she dozed off, her cheek lolling against his thick mat of hair. They skirted the walls of monasteries, rested on benches, met hikers on their path. One time, when they were caught in a sudden downpour, Vollard heaved his shoulder against the door of a forest cabin to open it. He lit a fire, recited fables and mimed the flight of large birds of prey.

But Éva said not a word. A shadowy figure behind a screen of frosted glass, captive in an ice-bound wasteland.

One day they came across some white monks in their habits, they too maintaining their silence as they moved about under the trees with their baskets, bending low over roots and dead leaves.

For Vollard, Éva became "la petite Chartreuse", a nun of the Carthusian order. Silent with no need to take a vow. A very small, very pale nun. A cloistered child. A child bereft of speech and joy, bereft of childhood. And yet, as he roamed the Grande Chartreuse in the company of the little girl, it was not the hideous absurdity of the accident that affected Vollard, but rather an inexplicable sense of appeasement, of relief and solace by dint of their ritual strolls in the stillness replete with small marvels. How could so small a creature, while vouchsafing so few signals, give him this impression of unassuming equilibrium, of fragile but happy urgency? The sense of purpose he had felt in the days of shuttling between the bookshop and the hospital intensified, now that he was going back and forth between the rehabilitation centre and the countryside with Éva for company. He was aware that it could not last. This bond was as tenuous as a wisp of smoke, he could foresee how it would end, for he knew the little girl was not mending, that she would never get well again, that miracles are no more than a blend of trickery and chance.

He wished for nothing more than to pass some days of his life in the company of the child, going for walks in the pollen-heavy sunshine, the splendour of these meadows and forests. The sensation of her small hand in his made him feel his own body less cumbersome, and when he went home, alone in the flat over the shop, he was better able to deal with his insomnia, and the war between the monologues of dread and the sentences in his head eased off. Drifting into sleep towards dawn one day, he dreamt that he was up on the mountain, walking alone in a maze of grey rocks, that he had lost the little girl and was searching for her, calling her name.

Éva became the child he had never had and would never have by any woman. The joyous blossoming of Vollard's desiccated seed: "Yes, joy! the joy I would have felt had I . . . the joy of being able to say 'my child', of thinking 'my son, my daughter' . . . my child right here by my side, close to me, trusting me . . . falling asleep while I watch over it . . . falling asleep with a shawl between its fingers, or a soft toy bald with age. My child lying here, breathing . . . I touch its smooth cheeks, the downy neck . . . my child needs me as much as I need the mist of promise and renewal that it brings." The question is, do only people with children of their own realise they are a party to an everyday miracle of renewal of the world? Are they aware of the vigour embedded in childhood? Do they appreciate the might of this "yes" full of wonder and spirited play that welcomes consequences, the "yes" that floats on the surface of tragedy like the glimmer of new hope?

Éva grew also to be the child that Vollard himself had been or might have been in an irrevocable past. Childhood memories crept up on him, filling his mind with figments of "I remember". I remember swatting flies and lining up their bluish, blood-splattered corpses on the floor. I remember the wounded bird at the bottom of the garden, which we

[144]

finished off, more out of nervous curiosity than out of compassion, by holding its head under water in the pond. I remember lying wide-eyed in the pitch darkness expecting something to spring from the door of the wardrobe which I knew to be ajar. I remember a day of flu and fever, spent alone tucked under a blanket, reading a story in which it was snowing thick and fast. Beguiled by the words "It was snowing", I suddenly looked up from my book as though alerted by an eerie silence, and saw that it was snowing outside too, as if by magic there was snow falling in the streets, turning the whole town white. The power of a story! The world transfigured by snow and by words. I remember long moments of immobility, moments of watchfulness frozen in childhood. I remember the precarious stature of that clumsy, ever-growing body, and the loneliness behind the glasses as thick as a submarine's portholes. The sickening memory of fearful distraction behind a protective barrier of solitude.

As long as the outings continued, the ghosts of childhood stalked Vollard, as if it was in Éva's power to call them up and exorcise them. The longer Éva remained silent, the closer they became.

When planted upright, the little girl had a way of rocking very gently from one foot to the other, her head tilted forward, blank look, arms hanging limply or crossed, the dark fringe lifting in the breeze. Or she would just sit with her hands flat on her thin thighs, with an air of utter unconcern. There were times when she stooped to pick up a pebble, which she held to her mouth and then dropped for no reason; times when she pulled the petals off daisies; and when, with Vollard to guide her, she tore open the green corsets of poppies to release the pleated scarlet buds; and when her hands made a tiny cage for agitated crickets.

It was at such times that the ghosts of childhood hovered around old Vollard. Ghosts of an anonymous, obscure childhood. A childhood unspecified in time and place, which he looked back on without nostalgia or regret. But he also knew that these walks in the Chartreuse, this spell of lightness in his existence, would come to an end. The little girl's strength was waning. She could not take more than a few steps before having to stop to get her breath back, her face twisted with soundless pain that seemed to be eating away at her, emaciating her, turning her the colour of wax.

The staff at the centre lamented Éva's almost complete anorexia, and Vollard took to bringing her fruit, chocolate, preserves each time he visited, but the child would eat nothing. She was wasting away.

One day, a few minutes after they set out on their walk, which nowadays amounted to the briefest of turns in the park, the little girl suffered a strange crisis. Her eyes rolled, turned inward, she lost her balance, subsided in slow motion to the ground. All Vollard could do was rush to the infirmary, cradling the almost inanimate creature in his arms. He had time to notice the white foam running from the lips on to his sleeve, and that she seemed to weigh nothing at all.

"Epileptic seizure," the doctor diagnosed, while the

[146]

deputy director, stifling another yawn, expressed concern at the mother's infrequent visits.

Vollard could see that over the past long weeks Thérèse Blanchot had come entirely to rely on him. She had charged him with the role of father, loving old uncle, or generous godfather to Éva, while all the time there was another man somewhere in the world, probably not even aware of being Éva's father, going about his business.

Thérèse had visited only twice, both times briefly, but she had telephoned regularly, timidly asking for news in the knowledge that the man from "The Verb To Be" was taking her daughter out for walks. But she did not appreciate that the forest air of the Chartreuse, the clean moist air of this mountain range with its ravines into which the torrents boomed, was not having the desired effect on the sick, mute child, the child with the damaged head.

Abruptly, without quite knowing why, Vollard heard himself telling the doctor and the deputy director, in the gruff tones of exasperated resolve, that he would track down this mayfly mother, make plain to her her daughter's condition, and persuade her whether she liked it or not to spend more time with Éva, at any rate such time as was left. He left the centre, set on finding Thérèse Blanchot and divesting himself of his ridiculous acting fatherhood. He mused upon the powdery gist of childhood that he had not known how to stop from slipping through his thick fingers.

The Oblivion of Books

Thérèse had to be found as soon as possible. That was what he kept telling himself. He had to let her know how very sick her little girl was. Convince her to come back and not to rush off again so quickly.

Vollard knew where the shopping mall was where Thérèse claimed she had found a job, but he did not recall (had she actually told him?) what kind of job it was. Checkout girl, hairdresser, sales assistant? Or had she found work in a bar? A hostess? Éva had been so weak when he last saw her. He knew she would get still weaker, that she was fading, slipping away. Driving down the mountain he tried not to think of the myriad little sensations he had shared with the child, but in spite of himself he kept hearing the plop of pebbles being thrown into the water, the creak of branches in the silence, the woodpecker drilling the bark of a tree, and he still felt the soft warmth of the child's hand in his. It was infuriating. With everything he had been through, with all those years behind him, an injection of sentimentality was the last thing he needed.

Back in the city, turning into the little square of "The Verb To Be", he knew at once from the wholly abnormal activity that another disaster had taken place.

"Fire? Where? A bookshop?"

Vollard pushed through the small crowd of bystanders, who were coughing from the last billows of thick smoke subsiding on to the pavement awash with streams of water. The acrid smell assaulted his nostrils, his lungs. Vollard saw that the doors to "The Verb To Be", barely discernible in the smoke, had been smashed, and that the floor of the darkened interior was now a murky pool with pages trailing on the surface like water plants.

Some firemen were already rolling up the hose, while others, booted and helmeted, were busy in the back of the shop shifting lumps of charred, sopping matter. Vollard sought out the captain, who referred him to the police officers still on the scene. Calmly one of them explained what had happened, as if, the sequence once set in train, the outcome was inescapable.

"Faulty wiring somewhere near your electricity meter. It was probably a spark that set fire to some plastic packing material. It had been quietly smouldering for some time, generating the black smoke that spread all over the store and stuck to all the books, the walls, absolutely everywhere in fact, and it was the awful stink that gave the alarm. Talk of luck! Lucky for the building, not to mention the whole neighbourhood. Just as well there were no flames! But something must have been combusting slowly for hours . . ."

So it hadn't even been a full-blown, glorious conflagration, Vollard thought. During his bad dreams in the early hours he had sometimes seen "The Verb To Be" on fire: an enormous, crackling bonfire of books with showers of sparks, a scene of dread and wonder. But the disaster that had just taken place had been more insidious, more ugly: a slow, smothered combustion accompanied by a thick cloud of soot that had percolated through the shop during the entire afternoon, covering everything and getting into everything, even between the pages of the books. The slime of a venomous toad had corroded the words and the phrases, returning each text to the inky bog of its origins. No single book in the shop had been spared.

In their hurtling passage to hose the back of the shop, the firemen had knocked over the display tables. Upturned boxes of old books lay soaking in the filthy water. The printed word had not surrendered to the cruel incandescence of an auto da fé: it had sunk piteously into an indeterminate, synthetic slush, a snowfall of mourning blotting out everything ever written, a collective winding-sheet, a coating of plasticised filth for the intellectual corpus of thousands of writers.

"That's how it is!" Vollard turned to find Madame Pélagie at his side, muttering these words over and over between clenched teeth. The neighbours had phoned, and she had come running. She had seen everything, the breaking down of the door, the hosing of the books. Her expression was earnest and careworn as usual, but very calm.

"You know, Étienne, the entire stock is ruined. Completely ruined, reduced to pulp. My account books are ruined, too, and so are the files. Everything!"

And she reached out this way and that to pick up stray

books, trying vainly to wipe them clean with her sleeve and then tossing them away among the debris of dissolved print.

The power had been cut, and in the firemen's searchlights Vollard's shadow loomed hugely over the devastation. He waded through what had once been his cave, his shell upholstered with phrases, all the way to his armchair, dirtied but intact, and his big table, overturned. Some of the authors' photographs on the wall had been spared. Their features were still recognisable under their coating of soot. Their eyes, like dimmed lights on the far side of remote misfortunes, were still there in spite of everything.

Madame Pélagie dithered about in the dark. Between her and Vollard there had never been any outward signs of affection – rather, a respectful distance. Polite reserve. No-nonsense. Just the ritual exchanges: "Ah, is that you, Étienne?" or "I'm off, Madame Pélagie . . . Don't know how long I'll be . . ." "That's fine, fine. You know I'll take care of everything," and then softly, between her teeth, but loud enough for Vollard to hear: ". . . as per usual."

But on the Sunday of the fire that was not a fire, when the daylight took for ever to fade and the oglers for ever to disperse, spoiled of their excitement, when the firemen drove off in their enormous red engine with a farewell blast of the siren, Vollard, in his sopping shoes and his clothes covered in revolting soot, put his hand on tiny Madame Pélagie's shoulder. She did not tilt her head against Vollard's arm, and he did not draw her close; they just stood there, she with her arms crossed, he breathing noisily, side by side confronting the extent of the damage. And yet, she did give the bookseller's thick fingers a fleeting caress.

Later on, Madame Pélagie, who had rarely if ever visited Vollard at home, accompanied him up to the flat, and they drank together, sitting silently across the kitchen table into the night. With the back of his hand Vollard had swept aside the books, which suddenly struck him as unnaturally intact, to make room for bottles and glasses. They took long draughts of red wine, unable to ignore the fact that they were directly above the devastated bookshop, so overpowering was the smell from downstairs.

After one long stretch of silence, Vollard said simply: "I think the little girl is going to die."

Madame Pélagie's head was filled with visions of books floating in a sea the colour of ink. She made an effort to replace them with the pale face of a child, wordless, ill, a child who was dying. She succeeded.

"I'm going down to put a padlock on the doors," Vollard said. "It'll take a long time for the water to drain away. I'll deal with the practicalities tomorrow. But I shall start looking for the mother as soon as I possibly can. I must! Do you remember the woman who came to see me in the shop? Just stood there and waited, never even glanced at the books, you told me yourself . . ."

"I remember. Strange young woman."

"Why don't you go home for now and rest, Madame Pélagie. This time, I promise to take care of everything."

"Well, this time I'll take you up on your offer."

Vollard spent a horrible day dealing with insurance people come to assess the damage, technical experts who were shocked by the decrepitude of the electrical installation, and clearance specialists also, to remove the detritus. But the detritus consisted of books with pages coalescing in soft, bloated forms.

From one ruined item to the last, Vollard cut short the formalities. He was in a hurry to get away, to seek out the woman he thought of as "Madame Blanchot" or "the child's mother", the woman who had prompted the deputy director to remark: "a proper will-o'-the-wisp, that lady", and of whom Madame Pélagie had prophesied: "a soap bubble, believe you me, Étienne, a bubble drifting along until all of a sudden, pop! nothing left, all gone! You mark my words . . . "

Taking the autoroute, he drove a hundred kilometres or more. One or two bombshells flew by and gave him the feeling of not making any headway at all.

From what Thérèse Blanchot had told him, the shopping mall he had to look out for was a vast lake of concrete covered with huge hangars full of merchandise, stores topped with glaring panels, parking lots, petrol stations, all spread out on the outskirts of the second largest town in the region. Thinking he had arrived, Vollard turned off the autoroute and nosed his van in among the thousands of other parked vehicles.

Huge fluorescent slogans leapt out at him, words blown

up out of all proportion yet insubstantial, like a bodybuilder's newly acquired muscles. Words taking possession of all that space with a cheerful violence. Vollard's van crawled ahead among thickets of signs. The vehicles were already tightly packed, and more kept arriving. No doubt there were glowering looks behind the tinted windscreens, hands keeping a stranglehold on steering wheels or gear sticks. Bumpers like sharks' jaws. But most awesome of all, on the forecourts of the superstores, were the teeming crowds of weary spectral shoppers trundling their overflowing carts or wandering aimlessly, under the eyes of CCTVs and guards with watchdogs, among the ghastly images of domestic bliss.

Finding a parking space at last, Vollard headed off towards the mall, and there observed at first hand the crowd performing the rites of mass acquisition, fingering the goods on display, desperately grabbing one article after another to add to their loot, all for one swipe of plastic at the checkout.

While Vollard scrutinised every brightly uniformed young woman in sight, he could not help spelling out the luminous signs and listening to every word of the tannoyed special offers. He read, in spite of himself, the oversized words splashed on billboards and on placards slung from the ceilings.

He was so disconcerted by this profusion of signals that he forgot that he was there to find Madame Blanchot. He was keeping an eye open, certainly, but he allowed himself to be carried away by this very simple, indiscriminate reading. Having arrived with his mind clouded and his heart heavy, Vollard let himself be buoyed up by this unexpected, but entirely tolerable, lightness. He even felt a kind of exhilaration in letting all these advertising slogans fill his eyes, his head. The longer he lingered among the shoppers, the more he felt a strange peace come over him. As if he had passed to the other side of the wall of pure disillusionment, the wall of anxiety. To a feeling of appeasement – limitless, multicoloured appeasement.

Sure, he was looking for Thérèse Blanchot, but suddenly he felt himself floating, pleasurably swimming in something like nothingness. A paradoxical nothingness, for there it was, right there in front of him, in all its glory. Hundred per cent nothingness. Uncomplicated nothingness. No history, no fuss. An illusory, undemanding entity.

When a trolley piled high with shopping and pushed by a sleepwalker bumped into his ankle or his thigh he was not in the least put out – on the contrary, he waved dismissively as if to say all's well, no harm done, sorry to have got at all in the way of the smooth passage of humankind and its shopping trolley.

At the same time he perfectly knew that he needed to be methodical if he was to find the Blanchot woman with the least delay and tell her about Éva, little girl lost in the silent forest, fading and dying miles away, there, up there in the Chartreuse.

An urgent voice murmured: "You must find the child's

mother," but this sane instruction evaporated in the quieting activity of strolling among the words and the merchandise. The voice had just as little effect as the one whispering into Thérèse Blanchot's ear: "Today you must get to the school on time," or "Éva's your daughter, remember, and you ought to behave like a proper mother."

It was Vollard's turn to become transparent, blissfully deciphering everything that caught his eye, awash with the sense that nothing matters, not really.

He pulled himself together. How would he recognise her? He started by dividing the women in the mall into two kinds: the ones labelling and stacking merchandise, and the ones filling their carts. But Thérèse? He had not paid enough attention that time she came to see him at the bookshop. Checkout girl? Sales assistant? Hairdresser? Waitress? Did it make any difference?

A great mellowness came over Vollard. A sentiment that was very relaxing in its banality. His mission had all the time in the world, and all the space. Dutifully he scanned the crowd as he roamed the mall, but he was all too willing to soak up the tepid soup of treacly music and saccharine words. The old bookseller was like a dazed bull shambling round the ring.

Inside the windows of bright-lit hairdressing salons there were girls with small tired faces. In the wide-open, noisy bars there were young women handling glasses, money, cigarettes. Sitting behind tinkling cash registers, other women in colourful uniforms ticked off all manner of items from their magic carpets, items covered in wonderful inscriptions waiting to be decoded.

None of these women was Thérèse Blanchot, but they all bore some resemblance to her. Same everywhere!

So Vollard trailed on, gorging himself on the phrases that were so deliciously bland, so gratifying. He was nowhere. Satiated. His eyes rolled in their sockets like a drunken bird's when they lit on the word "Bookshop" in pink letters on a blue ground. Between a row of television sets broadcasting images of reptiles in close-up on one side and a mass of fashion jewellery on the other, there was an array of merchandise that undeniably had the appearance of books. Vollard was dumbfounded. He could have stopped, could have turned to pick up a volume at random. He did neither. Had no desire to. The books were as foreign to him as the greenish reptiles lurching about on the screens.

He was set on carrying on as before, drifting pleasurably on the surface of a void. Alone unto himself, in a paradise of words frothing and bursting like bubbles.

It was at that exact moment that Thérèse darted towards him, panting, her hand to her chest.

"Monsieur Vollard, I saw you go past a while ago. I ran after you. Someone bumped into me and I lost sight of you. There are so many people here. It's me you're looking for, isn't it?"

Vollard did not know what to say. He twisted his face into a smile to hide his confusion at what he took to be a fortuitous encounter. There was a sharp edge to the coincidence, for it dragged him forcibly from his happy pottering, from the humdrum stupor that had magically purged his head of the old sentences.

Thérèse talked, talked too much: the remission had been short-lived.

"I've finished my shift. I work at a place called Nuptialand: eight hundred square metres of wedding frocks, wedding accessories, can you imagine?"

Vollard tried to imagine it, repeating the word Nuptialand in his mind, savouring it.

"I know you've come to tell me about Éva. I rang them up a few days ago: she isn't at all well. Every day I tell myself I'll give up this job and rush over there to go and see her, to do something, whatever. But I keep putting it off."

The salesgirl and the bookseller were walking side by side in the shifting shadows. Thérèse had linked arms with Vollard, who was absorbed in contemplation of the wondrous blood-red letters silhouetted against the sky and bleeding into the gathering darkness.

"I phone for news more often than you think. And you remember, when she was at the hospital, I did what I could. Talk to her? But what could I say? I'm not like you: I have trouble with words, sentences . . . Still, I like that stuff, basically. I even write things down, things that interest me, in a notebook . . . I'm not much of a talker. Been on the road too much. Listen, this is something I wrote: 'My entire life is out of focus, like a blurry photograph.' You see, Monsieur Vollard, it's not that my life is so bad, it's just blurry, one big

[158]

blur. Too many places, too many people, too many men. All the same!"

Thérèse was hanging onto Vollard's arm with both hands, her feet almost off the ground. He was scarcely listening.

"I know. Éva could have been my lucky break, made me happy. That's what they say: having a child, for some women, changes everything. In my case, being a mother isn't easy. It's a mistake to think being a single mother is easy, you know. I was just a kid myself. A kid with a little kid of my own. And then there's always this fog all around me, in my head, too. Forever wanting to get away, to move on to new things, to . . ."

". . . run away?"

The frail young woman and the big man arrived at the iron footbridge over the autoroute. They climbed up the steps and walked to the middle of the bridge with the rush of speeding cars beneath them. Huge trucks laden with goods destined for the mall thundered past, forcing Thérèse to raise her voice to a shout.

Vollard leaned back against the rusty railing and the young woman, on an impulse, pressed against him, gripping his lapels, as though set on climbing Mount Vollard.

"I want you to know that it's really important to me that you came today. It's a sign!"

"A sign? Well, as to that, we're being bombarded with signs every second," Vollard said. "A snowfall of signs. White ones, black ones."

[159]

"Still, you came, and I know you aren't like the rest, like other men, I mean."

"Do you carry on like this with every man you meet?"

"Of course not, you're different . . . Strong. Far away and yet very close. I don't know . . . and then I think of everything you've done for Éva."

"Running her over, for example? Fracturing her skull? Making her lose the power of speech for the rest of her life?"

Lifting her face to Vollard, Thérèse cried in despair: "Please, I beg you, don't leave me. Don't go away."

She buried her face in the chest of this man who was immense and heavy like a boulder, nuzzled into his armpit, but she did not weep because she did not know how.

"Calm down! You're shaking," Vollard said simply, gently drawing her close. Then he glanced around. "It's not at all cold, you know. Why don't you try and see how calm everything is: the roads going in all directions, the stores, the car parks, the billboards. Everything seems unfinished and finished at the same time. Finished at last! Unfinished for ever! Look, it's snowing! It's snowing signs and they don't mean a thing."

Thérèse snuggled up to him. Despite the mild air, she was shivering. Without a word, Vollard took off his jacket, the same jacket he had wrapped around Éva, and hung it round the shoulders of the young woman.

His only concern was to shield a fragile creature from the cold, but then, against all expectation, he had to admit that it was not a lost child that he was holding close, but a grown

[160]

woman, a woman whose touch, whose warmth and scent threw him into confusion.

It had been so long since such sensual electricity had travelled at such speed across his skin to his belly.

A woman's flesh against his chest, a woman's hair touching his lips, a woman's fingers clutching his shirt! After that soothing stroll in the void it felt like a delectable low punch delivered by a silken fist, a flood of desire returning from the past – but which past? Desire to tear away clothing, touch pale breasts, hold a minute existence in his hands, tenderly embrace a body eager to be embraced, pull the strings of the fairytale puppet, desire to give her life and pleasure to the last shudder, the last drop of humanity shed in the ultimate impossibility of communion.

He lifted Thérèse Blanchot off the ground with effortless ease, lightweight Thérèse whose mouth was buried in Vollard's beard, whose teeth sought out Vollard's lips, whose legs were not long enough to clamp around Vollard's waist, whose arms were entwined round Vollard's neck.

There was the brief moment, unforeseeable and absurd, of confusion, or fusion, between two creatures who should never have met. Then they hovered for a time, motionless, over the industrial zone that was sinking into the shadows beyond.

Locked in this embrace, Vollard progressed slowly across the footbridge. A gibbon in a grey jungle with its infant clamped under its belly, but equally a male mating with the fragile female of a different species, on the hoof.

Nibbling, licking, stroking areas of bare skin, the book-seller bereft of a shop, the reader bereft of books, lumbered into the equivocal night. At the end of the footbridge lay a stretch of wasteland.

Reaching the depths of the darkness, the grotesquely androgynous, febrile creature subsided on to the ground, unfolded itself and rolled down a slope into a shallow ditch, a nook of blackened grass and indescribable refuse.

Afterwards they drew apart, straightened up without speaking, without anger, and walked away in opposite directions.

To each their desert, to each their private snowfall.

The next day Thérèse headed for the centre where Éva lay dying, erasing her existence with child-like simplicity. Until the very last, until the imperceptible last breath, the mother stayed with her child, talking to her a little, now and then finding words.

With Éva dead, Thérèse made off, as far and as fast as she could go. She never saw Vollard again. It is unlikely that she ever heard how he met his death.

After the evening when he tracked down Thérèse and parted from her in the dark wilderness, Vollard the book-seller had gone back to the medical centre one more time. It was in the autumn. He was on his way across the park when someone told him that Madame Blanchot was at the little girl's bedside. He had turned tail.

He strove to forget the little girl, the wasted body, the

pallor, the unmoving lips, and was left with the awareness of the brevity of this childhood, which was all the more fleeting for having come into his life.

The sentences started up again at the back of his skull, but he had stopped paying attention to them. Double-talk. Nonsense.

The premises of "The Verb To Be" were put up for sale, and shortly afterwards were converted into a hairdressing salon. The floor of what was once a forest of books was laid with gleaming tiles, on to which, from then on, tufts of shorn human hair would come to fall under the click-clack of the hairdressers' little shears.

The former bookseller had kept his old flat, but almost daily he went for a drive along the dizzying bends of the Chartreuse. He walked for hours along the footpaths. He drove in his van, quite aimlessly. That is how, one day towards evening, he found himself approaching the skeletal bridge from which he had taken that lunatic elasticated jump into the ravine.

His head, his limbs, his gut had preserved the memory of vertigo and the subsequent thrill edged with nausea. The terror and the drop. The failed escape from the labyrinth.

On that autumn evening, at the end of a beautiful day shimmering with blue, silver, yellow and russet, there was no-one on the bridge. Vollard turned off the engine, waited for a moment, then stepped out of his van. The slam of the car door reverberated eerily from the rock faces. The depths were already in deep shadow, but way up above, huge birds circled in a sky still tinged with gold. Vollard walked silently, listening to the distant roar of the torrent coursing between the shiny black boulders. Leaning out over the abyss, he perceived the rocks to be the humped backs of mammoths burying their heads in the mud and foam. The wind whistled around him. A desolate spot, this cleft in the Chartreuse. Empty and pointless in the absence of the good-looking, muscular youngsters with tanned faces who made a pretence of throwing themselves into the void but who succeeded with such apparent ease in living.

Vollard walked on until he was in the middle of the bridge. The shadows were spreading apace. Not a car in sight. No-one would be taking this little-frequented road before morning.

He stood for a moment with his elbows propped on the parapet, and in the silence of the mountain that breathes the same sense of loneliness as the roar of an autoroute, Vollard became aware of one particular sentence circling round him like a bitch in heat: ". . . *the privation of contact would, I knew, be my downfall in the end, in the same way as it once was both a necessity and a good thing . . .*"

Then another sentence made itself heard, and another, then some more, ghostly and timid at first, and Vollard had no doubt that the burbling mass would seethe and spread from one moment to the next to trouble his new-found rest. Suddenly, with astonishing agility, he swung one leg over the parapet, then the other, and sat on the edge of the void. Down in the deepening obscurity the great black beasts shifted their rumps, hunched their mighty shoulders in the silvered foam of the torrent, and gradually turned into books, unrecognisable, shut tight.

Bookseller Vollard, without taking his eyes off the depths, drew himself up to his full height on the parapet as he had done that memorable day when he was strapped into a harness and roped into a giant elastic band, the day when he had dropped over the edge only to bounce up high and drop and rebound again.

He felt a bit giddy. He could still hear the muffled refrain of the familiar sentences, but he could no longer tell whether they were erupting in his chest, unfurling at the back of his head or rising up from the falling water like a noxious spume.

"Now both legs were hanging outside and he had only to let go of what he was holding on to — and he was saved. Before letting go he looked down . . . at the instant when icy air gushed into his mouth, he saw exactly what kind of eternity was obligingly and inexorably spread out before him."

The bitch of a sentence grovelled and fawned, adapting herself as well as she could to the situation.

A bird of prey uttered a long shriek, like a newborn babe, a dying infant. Vollard stepped forward.

His last step into the abyss swirling with all that has been written, all that is given unto man to read.

His first step into the oblivion of books.

Thanks are due to the writers whose works, wholly or in part, inhabited the memory of Étienne Vollard: André Breton, the Gospel According to St John, Goethe, Nietzsche, Pier Paolo Pasolini, Victor Hugo, Malcolm Lowry, Georges Bataille, Samuel Beckett, Henri Michaux, Fernando Pessoa, Jorge Luis Borges, Pierre Loti, Nathalie Sarraute, Adalbert von Chamisso, Jean de La Fontaine, Thomas Bernhard, Vladimir Nabokov.

www.randomhouse.co.uk/vintage